Beached in a Camper

Three Weeks Surviving an Older Brother,
Bug Bites, Water Bombs and a Girl

To: Jake and Eli

Moynihan

2013

Written and Illustrated by
Kate Moynihan

ISBN-10: 0615797334
EAN-13: 9780615797335
Library of Congress Control Number: 2013907051
CreateSpace Independent Publishing Platform
North Charleston, South Carolina

Dedication

This book is dedicated to my mom and dad who made camping possible. To my two sons who made these stories possible. To all of them for allowing me to exaggerate and make this fun fiction possible.

Acknowledgements

I am most grateful for the help of my friends and mentors: Nicole Brace, Allison Dempkey, Mark Lewison, Donna Stack, Christina Streeter, Paul VanKolken, and my husband, Larry Weller.

Table of Contents

Chapter 1

Starting Out with a Bang

I dart past campsite marker Number 26, running faster to cover more ground. I look left, no luck. I glance right, nothing. Where can it be? Heat sizzles up from the blacktop path that bakes under the blazing summer sun. My sweaty head itches under the baseball cap, but that is not important. What's important is to find it.

"Over here!" yells my brother, Brian, who is ten years old to my nine.

I spin around, following the sound of his voice. Across the campground, a metal post gleams in the sun. There it is! The water spigot – king of the campground.

"Yes!" I say as I whip off my ball cap and wave it in the air victory-dance style. I dash over to Brian.

Truth is, tent campers simply use the spigot for a water supply. But today, Brian and I have other plans.

"Grab the pack of - - " Brian says, yet before he can finish his sentence, I'm off to the camper.

My name is Adam Moynihan and having set up camp only minutes earlier, I know exactly where to search. After yanking open the screen door, it bangs behind me as it slaps against the side of the metal camper. I hop over the two-step entrance, slide down the narrow aisle, and smack into the kitchen sink. It's tight quarters in the camper.

My quick moves cause Mom's head to spin, sending her shoulder length brown hair swinging.

"Slow down!" Mom says.

"But Brian's waiting and I gotta grab the balloons!"

"Were they on the must-have list?" she asks.

"You bet."

"And you remembered to pack them?"

I freeze. Did I forget? Just yesterday I forgot to return a library book. But I couldn't have forgotten the balloons.

Quickly, I punch the latch on a lower cupboard in the back corner of the camper. My cupboard. Mom assigns Brian and me a cupboard each – like a school locker – to store our special things. I tug the drawer open, snag my backpack, and flip open the secret pocket. Empty. How could I have forgotten balloons? Every summer, I camp with Mom and Brian at Muskegon State Park in West Michigan and water balloons rule at this place.

Fearing the unthinkable, I poke at every corner of the pocket but find nothing. My legs wobble and go soft as Play-Doh. I slump onto the bench seat in the kitchen.

"Looking for these?" Mom asks.

I raise my head and see in her hand a clear plastic bag full of red, green, and blue balloons.

"Huh? How did you end up with them?" I ask, amazed.

"They were left in the grocery sack," she says.

"Gee, thanks," I say. "I guess this gives me one more spot."

"That's right, your forgetfulness is as certain as a leopard's spots." Her bright blue eyes seem to laugh at being in on the joke.

"Gotta go." I snatch the balloons from Mom, who then sneaks in a quick kiss on the noggin. Our leopard pun always gets me that little peck on the top of my head. Mom likes the mushy stuff. With Dad, it would have been a thump on the shoulder or a big bear hug like I got from him when I said goodbye this morning.

Brian and I live nearby at Dad's house in Spring Lake, Michigan. Sometimes it feels sad to leave Dad and visit Mom, but not right now. There are balloons to fill. Water bombs to make!

In a flash, I am back at the water spigot with Brian. I pull out the rainbow colored balloons.

"I'm older, so let me stretch the balloon onto the spout," my brother says.

3

"Go ahead," I say, slapping a balloon into his hand. One year older isn't that much more.

"Besides, I know a trick," Brian says. "If you pull the stem a few times, the rubber relaxes." He snaps the balloon stem twice and easily stretches it over the spout.

"Yeah, well, wait till you see me tie the knot," I say. "Remember I've been practicing knot tying with gummy worms."

"Except you ate so many worms you hardly had any left to practice with." Brian's mouth curls up and he snickers.

"I've had enough practice! Just wait and see," I bark back, my face burning. Why do I let his smart remarks get to me? I reach for the faucet ready to blast it on, full force.

"Turn it on slowly or it'll rip the stem," Brian says, grabbing my wrist. He must have X-ray vision and can see the energy surge through my fingers wanting to crank that spigot hard.

"All right already. I'll turn slowly," I say.

Brian is the human "pause button" that saves me from trouble. More than once, he has kept me from crashing, smashing, or getting blown to bits while playing video games and on occasion, in real life, too.

I gently turn the knob, water oozes in and the balloon slowly swells. I tap my foot, waiting. The sound of trickling water lulls my eyes closed and sends me into fantasyland. Suddenly, I am Batman, the master crime fighter. From my belt filled with superpower weapons, I whip a bat-a-rang boomerang into the air. Then I dart ahead, my black cape snaps ...

"Adam, pay attention!" Brian yells, his voice startling me.

I blink and zero in on the balloon. Whoa. It's bursting-full and wiggly now, cradled in Brian's hands under the faucet. I squat, eye-to-eye with the balloon, hand steady on the faucet.

"Hold still ... almost there ... that's perfect," I say.

I turn off the water and peel the balloon stem from the spigot. I stretch the stem with all the finger strength I built from practicing with gummy worms. I whip the stem around two fingers, pull it through and – zip! It's tied.

"See? Faster than you can tie your shoes," I say, shoulders back and head held high.

"Okay, whiz kid, focus on another one," Brian says.

Soon we have a jiggly pile of red, green, yellow and blue balloons. Of course, this attracts kids from nearby campsites. In fact, there are more kids here now than were in my fourth grade class. With an eagle eye, I scan the packed crowd hoping to find a familiar face. It's the same season of cut-offs and campfire fun I was crazy about when we were here with Mom back in June. Now it's August, and I am here for three more weeks.

"Do you see anyone you know?" I ask Brian.

"I don't think so," he says, giving the crowd of kids a once-over.

"Nobody?" I ask.

"I'm pretty sure," Brian says with a shrug. He returns his focus to stretching the last unfilled balloon into place.

Cripes. I thought I'd find a few friends from back in June. Now, an uneasy feeling creeps over me, like being the new kid at school. My breath catches in my throat. Will these kids like me?

I'm kind of an in-the-middle kid. My last name is M for Moynihan, right in the middle. And the color of my green eyes is in the middle. Not dark like emeralds, not light like play money. And no matter how hard I work to get my baseball pitch to curve, it stays in the middle. I wonder if these kids will like ordinary, middle me.

Once more I check out the crowd of kids standing around stiff as statues and watching the water balloons. "Sure is a quiet group," I say to Brian.

"They certainly are." He steadies the last balloon on the spigot while I control the water flow.

Suddenly, a girl with a face full of freckles bulldozes through the crowd and levels a little red-haired boy as she beelines for the balloons.

"Yeeouch!" The boy takes a nose dive to the ground.

"Quit pushing, Freckles," I say to the girl, not knowing her real name.

"I'm on a mission, Sweetie," Freckles says, her eyes laser-focused on the pile as she comes full speed ahead for the balloons.

"You need to stay back." Determined to keep her from the balloons, I let go of the faucet and stretch my arms out like a school crossing guard.

"Not likely, Sweetie," she cautions.

Freckles keeps plowing forward and tries to grab a balloon.

I wrap my arms around her. "Stay back," I say.

She squirms and tries to break free. Freckles is about my size but seems to have the power of Wonder Woman. It takes all my strength to keep her away from the stockpile of balloons.

"Adam, get back here!" Brian yells. "You need to turn off the water. Now!"

My eyes dart toward him. Oh no! The filling balloon is swollen to twice the size of the others. Orange rubber bulges beyond Brian's cupped hands. The running water is out of control, but what can I do? Whatever I decide, I need to do it quickly. Unsure, I keep one hand on Freckles and bend forward to grab the spigot.

My last ditch effort is too late. The orange balloon explodes! Brian is soaked – head to toe.

"Way to go, Adam," he says. The instant blast of cold water makes his whole body shiver, except his jaw, which is locked angry-tight.

I gasp at the sight of him. But seeing Brian dripping wet and covered in tiny specks of orange rubber makes me giggle. Then he gives me a death glare, scoops up a water balloon, raises his arm, and aims.

"Wait! Don't do it! Wait! Wait!" I beg.

"Fat chance," Brian says while spitting out a piece of balloon. I can tell he is in full pay-back mode, not pause-button behavior. Without hesitation, he heaves the balloon. Splat! The balloon smacks me in the chest and bursts like pop fizzing out of a shaken-up bottle.

Instantly, it is war! Hands grab for balloons. Whoosh. A blue bullet whizzes by my head. A green grenade soars past my shoulder. I dive for cover, land on my stomach, and protect my head with my hands. Splat! Pow! Like bombs, balloons explode from every angle. Squishy-wet gym shoes slosh all around me.

Nearby, I hear Freckles shout to the red-haired kid, "Hey, Sweetie. Heads up!"

That's when I figure out she calls everyone Sweetie. Taking a closer look, I see she's not wearing a simple T-shirt and shorts like the rest of us. Instead, she is dressed like a Barbie doll, wearing a bright pink dress and matching flip-flops. But her fancy outfit doesn't slow her down.

"Bombs away!" Freckles shouts. She fires with so much force it spins her in a circle, sending her brown pigtails whirling.

The little kid tries to duck, but the well-aimed balloon slams into his chest, bursting on impact and spraying him all over.

"Here's one more," Freckles says as she lets loose another speedball.

Before the little kid can blink, the balloon explodes on his head and soaks his baseball cap. His wet body shudders and his chin quivers. I wonder why she is picking on the little guy. In fact, her actions are in the ballpark of a double-dare. I can't walk away from a challenge like this.

Two balloons skid to a stop next to me, unpopped, and I capture one in each hand. "Hey Freckles, take this!" I blast the balloons at her skinny legs poking out from the fancy dress.

It's a double whammy as the two balloons burst and soak my target. Freckles stands frozen. Her eyes, a stormy sea green, land on me like a lighthouse beacon. She searches for another water bomb to sail my way, but all the balloons are destroyed. Her frigid eyes glare at me as she lets out a huff and marches off.

She isn't the kind of friend I would want, anyway. Or is she? A bit of a smile forms on my face. Come to think of it, Freckles is the one who started The Great Water Balloon War. This freckle-faced firecracker, who cooled us off on a hot summer day, might just be a friend after all.

Then, out of nowhere, a water bomb explodes all over on my back. I whirl around.

"Found one, Sweetie!" Freckles says, smiling wider than when you say "Cheese" for the camera.

I smile back and she wanders away. Feeling a tug on my shirt, I look down. It's the soaked little red-haired kid. I tip my ball cap to him. He tries to tip his but it drops in the sand.

"No harm done," I say, picking up the hat. I try to brush away the sand, but most of it just sticks to the soggy cap with a T-ball logo on it. "So, you play on a little tyke's baseball team?"

He nods yes as his shiny round eyes glisten, reminding me of little flying saucers. His soggy hair is stuck to his head except for one wild spike that shoots straight up like a Martian antenna.

After one last brush, I hand back the cap. "Good as new. Besides, the best part of camping is getting dirty."

The kid grins, his apple-like cheeks glowing red. Apparently, he is too bashful to talk. He slaps the soggy cap on his head and trots away.

Moments later, I catch up to Brian back at the water spigot. This time, he's not filling balloons. I watch him let the gushing water push clumps of sand out of his shoes. Muskegon State Park has miles of fine, soft sand all along the Lake Michigan shore.

"No 'singing sand' today," I say, using the term we "locals" use to describe the special beach sand here.

West Michigan sand particles are so tiny that when the sand is hot and dry, it screeches and squeaks a little "song" under your foot with each step.

"No chance you'll find any singing sand with all this water around here," Brian says. His wet shoes slap the blacktop path as we slosh our way back to the camper.

"That bunch of kids certainly caused a lot of fun," Brian says.

"Yeah, it was an awesome water balloon fight," I say.

"Do you have any balloons left?" Brian asks.

"Sure do." No reason to tell him that Mom was actually the one who remembered to pack the balloons. I just say, "They're small, so I was able to bring a lot." Small size is important when living in a camper with a pint-size kitchen and fold-out beds. Unlike my favorite superhero's Bat Cave, there are no hidden tunnels or caves for extra storage.

"Hey, Adam, I have an idea," Brian says. He rubs his hands together, which lets me know his mind is racing.

Uh-oh. Here we go. Sometimes Brian's ideas take a lot of brainpower, like they're homework or something.

"We should make a water balloon game and we can charge money to play," he says.

Boy, sometimes his ideas are really good. Better than recess. Grinning now, I think about all those rowdy kids who will bring money to pitch water balloons. Quickly, I do some numbers in my head. My brother's idea will make us rich!

Brian hustles over to the camper bike rack and tugs at the thick cardboard we squeeze in to keep the bikes from rubbing together on bumpy roads. "Grab the other end of this cardboard," Brian calls to me. "We can use this to build a carnival game like the bean bag toss at the Grand Haven Coast Guard Festival. We'll cut holes out of the cardboard for faces to peek out."

"Yeah, and instead of pitching bean bags, the kids will toss water balloons," I say, darting to Brian's side. We pull the bulky cardboard loose and lay the thick board on the ground.

"Let's see. First, I'll measure so the two holes are in the center of the target board," Brian says. My brother is certain to build a top-notch carnival game because he wins prizes at the Junior Science Fair. While I usually dream of being Batman, Brian could be Alfred

Pennyworth – the mastermind butler. Brian, like Alfred, knows the ins and outs of every gadget and contraption. He can make a volcano erupt foam even without using a science book.

"Well, you've got the game under control, but how will we let kids know about playing?" I ask.

"You can use Mom's laptop to make a sign," Brian says.

"Yeah, and we can hand them out to all the kids!" I reply as visions of being rich flash through my mind. I'll finally be able to buy an official Captain America shield. Captain America is my second-favorite character after Batman.

Eager to make the signs, I dash into the camper and dart toward the laptop. But then I stop dead in my tracks, remembering that there is no printer. You can only bring along the bare minimum when you go camping. Now what?

I hear Brian cutting the cardboard. He is going to be finished before I even get started. I plop on the couch, sinking low and feeling helpless, like a turtle stuck on its back.

Twirling my ball cap in my lap, I rub the Chicago Cubs logo. I thought this was my lucky cap because Alfonso Soriano almost signed it. Where is my good luck when I need it?

A minute drags by. Then five. Looking out the window, I see my brother cutting the second hole for another face to peek out from the target. I've got to do something. I drop my gaze a bit and catch sight of Mom's art paper. Mom earns her living as an artist, so art supplies are always included on the vacation must-have list.

"Hey, Mom," I call while heading outside to the picnic table. Mom is busy anchoring the corners of a tablecloth so we can eat lunch outdoors. I snuggle up to her the way she likes. "May I use some of your colored paper? Brian and I are making a water bomb – uh, balloon – game."

"I wondered what your brother was building." Mom looks away from the tablecloth and over to Brian's project with cardboard.

"Kids will pay money to play. We're going to be rich," I explain.

"Another money-making adventure?" she asks, eyebrows raised. Mom's eyebrows have a language all their own. Right now, those soft brown eyebrows seem to have their doubts.

"Yep. We'll make lots of money."

"Like selling blueberries last summer?"

"You bet. Just like it," I say. "Remember, after picking berries at Palmer's blueberry patch, Brian and I divided them up into your Tupperware dishes and sold them to other campers. We made tons of money."

"And the rest of the story?" Mom asks.

"Well, um." I forgot that Mom lost money on that deal. We never paid her for buying the berries at the farm or replacing the Tupperware. I lower my head and keep quiet. Sometimes it is best to stop short when you mess up. Let silence work its magic. Especially with Mom, I don't want to sugar coat the truth.

I gaze up at her, and notice a corner of her mouth tipping up into a smile. "The extra paper is in the back cupboard. Take what you need," she says.

Lucky me, the magic of silence worked. I should be able to have my signs made before Brian finishes the game board. I give Mom a hug and get a whiff of her Chanel No. 5 perfume. I know the name because Mom pointed it out in a TV commercial with a beautiful lady in diamonds and a mink coat. Mom's look got all starry-eyed over that. Just like me, Mom likes to daydream.

I hustle into the camper, pick the rainbow pack of construction paper and take it out to the picnic table. High above my head, skyscraper-tall trees swish in the breeze while I sit at the table, and my bare toes wiggle in the cool, shaded sand below. A fuzzy spider creeps at the edge of the table to study my work in progress. Ah, the wonders of working in the great outdoors.

Lost in thought about the signs, I don't see what's happening behind me. Then I hear a clang. What's that? My head turns toward the rattling sound. Empty pop cans roll and spin around Mom's feet.

"Oh, my. The raccoons found the recycle bag." She bends over and chases down empties as sticky syrup spills about. "My goodness, the mosquitoes are out, too," she says, swatting a biter on her arm.

It's funny how Mom doesn't see the same beauty in camping that Brian and I do. She'd rather be in the TV commercial, dripping in diamonds and wearing a mink coat. Yet, Mom sticks it out for us boys.

With the syrupy cans collected, she wanders over to the picnic table. "How are the signs coming along?" she asks.

"I'm trying to print neatly, but this is hard for me," I say.

"Are you printing better than on your spelling test?"

"I couldn't help it if the teacher thought my 'a' looked like an 'o.'"

Taking a deep breath, I settle back into my work and try to write straight and steady. But the tip of the pencil pushes too hard into the paper. It snaps. The lead bullet hits me between the eyes. I wrinkle my forehead to chase away the sting. Now there are only three sharp pencils left.

Seeing me struggle, Mom steps closer and says, "Here, I can help write a few." In only fifteen minutes, we finish a bundle of signs.

'Totally Soak a Face!'

Come to the Water Balloon Toss

*** 1 to 2 p.m. today at Campsite 21 ***

(only 10 cents a balloon)

The signs are done, and now I roll up each one like a tube and fasten it with a rubber band. Hmm. How will I deliver them to kids around the campground? My Magna mountain bike is a powerful 5-speed with wide dirt-bike tires. It's great to climb hills, but has only a water-bottle holder for storage, so it's not really cut out for sign delivery.

For a moment, I find myself wishing for my old Schwinn with its drop-down basket. I snap out of it when I remember it had training wheels! I'd look like a big dork sitting on that peewee bike, that's for sure. How do I come up with such goofy ideas?

I shake my head in thought. There must be a good delivery solution. Don't have a scooter. Don't have a wagon. I shove my hands in my pockets. That's it! I'm wearing the delivery answer – cargo shorts have lots and lots of pockets.

Quickly, I stuff rolled signs into every pocket; fronts, backs, and down each leg. I take a step ... and a sign drops out. I take another ... and another sign tumbles to the ground. It's a Hansel and Gretel bread-crumb trail of signs.

I hear someone giggling nearby and spot the little red-haired kid from the balloon war. He must have left his wet T-ball cap back at his camper – and now his hair has dried into a lion's mane of a wild mess. He runs his fingers through it, and it gets crazier. Even with his hair on end, this little guy only comes up to my chest.

"Do you own a comb?" I ask, knowing it probably wouldn't help. Besides, this is camping. A comb is for the school year.

Red shakes his head to say no. The kid is cute in an oddball way.

"How old are you?"

Red holds up an open hand.

"Five," I say. Shucks, he's little. I look around. There are no other kids in sight. Another sign tumbles out of my jam-packed pockets. If I want some delivery help, I'll have to settle for this little guy. "Would you like to deliver these signs with me?"

Red's mouth drops open, no words come out. But his eyes, round as baby beach balls, bounce up and down as he nods his head yes.

I hand Red some signs. It feels good to no longer be an overstuffed kangaroo.

We march along the blacktop path that circles the campground. Red waves the signs in the air and I call out to other kids, "Have a blast! Join the fun!"

Here and there out of nowhere, kids run toward us, curious about the signs.

"Ask your Mom. If she says no – then go ask your Dad. Don't miss out!" I sing out.

The kids race away to grab their coins for the 10 cent water balloons. "I can't wait to be rich," I say to Red.

He nods again, this time flashing a bigger smile that reveals he is missing both front teeth. It makes me grin. I bet that jingle in his pocket is from coins the tooth fairy left him.

"We'll be so rich. I can finally buy a Spiderman comic book," I say, giving name to my third-favorite superhero.

There is a happy skip in my step as we head back to camp.

"Look! Brian has cut the target holes out for the faces to peek through," I say.

Red's face lights up as he takes in the cardboard carnival game.

"Do you like it, Adam?" Brian asks. "I just finished painting the bull's-eye around each hole."

"It's great." Then I turn toward Red and say, "Too bad the painting part is finished. But don't worry, little guy. We'll get a chance to paint another time."

Red nods, and when his smile grows even wider, it shows twin dimples.

I must have a soft spot for this five-year-old because I invite him again. "My mom packs rolls of paper so long that we can paint a picture bigger than this picnic table."

Red points to a pile of bungee cords tangled at Brian's feet and looks at us questioningly.

"I'll be doing crisscross, bungee-cord engineering to anchor the game," Brian explains.

"Just watch him work," I say to Red. Brian hooks one end of a bungee cord through a corner slot he carved into the cardboard and then he stretches and wraps the other end around the picnic table. A second bungee hooks to an opposite corner slot in the cardboard and is tightened around a tree trunk.

"Almost magical, isn't it?" I say. Brian could win a blue ribbon with this over-under-crossway style.

By 1 p.m., the balloons are filled and piled high next to Brian's feet. He sits in a lawn chair, ball cap on his head and the money box cradled on his lap. We are ready for the carnival game. We are ready to get rich!

Having finished stacking balloons, I notice Red is still here. Red is so quiet, I sometimes forget about him. "How'd you like to be with me behind the game?" I ask.

Red doesn't even take time to nod his head. He darts behind the target board and pokes his head through one of the openings. I join him, peeking my head out the other hole.

"You look silly. All I see are your heads bobbing," Brian chuckles. "Hold on, here comes the first customer."

Brian wipes the smile from his face as a kid twice my size stomps up. I imagine the ground shakes like a number-eight earthquake. "Psst," I whisper to Red. "This kid is big enough to be the king of middle school."

Red nods and his mouth drops open as his eyes fix on the giant.

"Rrrghh," the big kid snarls at Brian and then he thrusts my brother a dime. The big kid's hat is pulled low. It covers most of his face, which makes him more mysterious. I hang onto the cardboard so tight my knuckles turn white.

The big kid grabs a red water balloon and his XXL hand completely covers it. He spits on the red balloon and rubs it between his hands. Squeak, squeak, the dry sand sings as he moves one bare foot around to gain traction for a throw. A wave of the willies shudders through me.

Warming up like a major league baseball pitcher, the kid swings his long throwing arm in a circle, then arches it behind his head. His arm muscle shows off big, stretching the fabric of his green T-shirt. It pulls so tightly, I imagine him busting out of his shirt and becoming the Incredible Hulk. My gut is saying "Get the heck out of here," but Red hangs tough, so I do too.

Hulk extends his arm farther back, and from the pressure of his mighty grip, the red rubber balloon squishes to pink between his clenched fingers. In one rapid motion, Hulk fires the balloon and it whips through the air.

Splat! Like a grenade, the balloon blows to bits when it smacks into the tree less than a foot from my head.

"He missed us, Adam!" little Red yells, finally finding his voice.

Whew. I wipe my sweaty forehead with my T-shirt. Round one, safe.

Hulk grabs a balloon for a second try. 'Round and 'round whirls his arm. I hold my breath and close my eyes. Swoosh! I hear the balloon whiz only inches over my head, then slam with a slosh into a tree right behind us. Water sprays on us in a brief shower, and we gasp in relief.

Round two, safe. Not bad.

Red looks at me and beams, as we're still mostly dry.

"Pitcher has a rubber arm ... rubber arm ... flubber arm!" Red sings. There isn't an ounce of shyness left in this little guy now.

"Look here, pal," Hulk says, his face now the color of that busted red balloon. With his fists clenched, he stomps toward Red and gets dangerously close to the kid.

Red sticks out his tongue at Hulk and then ducks his head out of the hole, taking cover behind the cardboard.

"How about one more chance?" Brian asks the Hulk to distract the big guy.

It works, and Hulk turns back toward Brian. He leans in so close to my brother that their faces are only inches apart. Hulk growls through gritting teeth, digs deep into one pocket, and flings his last dime at Brian.

"Thank you, sir," Brian says in his pause-button fashion and slowly tips his ball cap to Hulk, indicating all is cool.

Hulk snatches a balloon. Red cautiously pokes his head back through the target hole, and Hulk takes aim, this time closing one eye. After taking a deep breath, he fires his last balloon and lets out a wicked wail. The balloon bullets toward us.

Ka-boom! The balloon connects high on Red's forehead and water sprays in every direction. Silence for a second, and then Red sputters, "This is really cool!" Red spews more water and then shakes his head like a dog after a bath.

Hulk flashes a giant smile of victory and wanders away the conqueror. But the ground where he walks only shakes about a number three now on my earthquake meter.

Only a few more kids show up. Red stays busy, poking his head in and out of the opening. We don't get rich, but we do get a friend, and it is only our first day of camping.

Chapter 2

Duct Tape and Beyond

Suddenly I'm flying through the air and landing a belly flop in the sand. Just a second ago, I was strolling to the playground, but now I'm curled into a ball clutching my throbbing big toe. What did I trip over?

Brushing sand aside, I explore the spot and hit something hard and a little odd. I dig deeper to uncover a piece of smooth gray wood. "What's this?" I yell to Brian who waits up ahead near the swings with his arms folded and a can't-be-bothered look on his face.

Brian slowly shuffles back toward the vacant campsite where I fell. "Looks like wood left over from a fire. A camper probably left it behind," he says.

I yank the old plank out of the sand and stand it upright. The top of the board towers above my head and the width is chunky. My hand barely wraps around it.

"This isn't firewood," I say, thinking instead it could be the mast from a pirate ship. Instantly I daydream, seeing myself as the captain hoisting a skull and crossbones flag high in the air. I hear the flag snap in the wind and can smell the salty sea.

But just as suddenly, Brian takes the wind out of my sail. "The wood looks like a two-by-four that builders use for construction," he says as he studies the uniform width and depth of the long board. Then his eyes move to my foot. "Is your toe going to be okay?"

My big toe is getting puffy and starting to glow a bright red. Yet the initial bolt of pain that went straight to my eyeballs has lessened and I'm not seeing stars or anything. However, swinging from the monkey bars is out of the question. "I'll be okay. You can go to the playground without me."

"You should have worn shoes," Brian chirps in a Mom-advice way.

I wave my brother off and jab one end of the long board into the sand to use it like a crutch for a minute. I am usually a tough kid, but it's hard to be tough when your toe is turning red to purple.

"Why aren't you running off to the playground? Don't you want to make new friends?" I ask.

But instead of hustling to the playground, Brian doesn't budge. Instead, he stares at something behind me. He clears his throat and, with a teasing tone in his voice, says, "Well, well. Guess who's coming this way."

That's weird. We don't know many kids here because it's only our second day of camping. I turn slowly to balance my two-by-four cane and protect my injured toe.

It's Freckles. The girl who nailed me but good during the Great Water Balloon War. She whizzes by on a bike, her long, brown pigtail braids trailing behind her in the wind. She's dressed fancy again, including a frilly purse over her shoulder that bumps her hip as she pedals.

"It's your girlfriend, Adam," Brian snickers.

I stare daggers at him for that comment. "Just you wait," I say, stabbing my cane into the sand and taking a step toward him. A blast of pain tears through my toe. My angry step toward my brother becomes just a helpless hobble.

"Easy now," Brian cautions – but his mouth twists into a smile. I can tell he's ready to let loose with a belly laugh, but then he notices something over my shoulder. His keen green eyes scan the campsite area just beyond the unused fire pit. He takes a panther-like step, prowls the spot and then pounces on his prize – a bunch of cut up two-by-fours. "I was right! And these pieces are short enough to be used for firewood."

Brian's hunter know-how proves he's right, but the pounding in my big toe is too much for me to care.

"Look at all this firewood. I knew I was right," my brother tells me again.

I ignore him, and my silence works. He gets busy scooping up chunks of wood, and when his arms are chock-full he finally says, "Let's go back to camp."

Brian struggles under his load and I limp way behind. Now my toe is about twice its size, but when the pain lessens a bit, I realize I'm on the mend.

By the time I stumble into our campsite, Brian has already dumped the bundle of wood and is headed back to claim a second round. He returns with a board that is taller than his height of four feet, eight inches. "Look! I found another long two-by-four."

"That makes two long boards and a bunch of foot-longs," I say. "This is great! We've never had this much lumber to build with before." My mind wildly races with dreams about building things, including the perfect dog house for the pet I've always wanted. In a snap, I'm no longer focused on my painful toe.

"Let's make bookends," Brian says, naming one of our simple Cub Scout projects. Of course my brother would think of bookends. His love for reading has made his mind a walking encyclopedia.

"But Brian, look at all this lumber! We can build big! The heck with bird feeders or bookends," I say, my arms outstretched to show him just how big we can dream.

"Except for one thing." Brian's voice is quiet, yet certain.

"What's that?"

"Mom's toolbox."

I forgot Mom isn't much of a fixer upper. Her toolbox consists of one hammer and two screwdrivers.

"Remember the last time Mom tried to fix my skateboard wheel? She told me to pass her the 'thingamajig,'" Brian recalls.

"And she meant pass the duct tape," I immediately say to finish Brian's statement. We both chuckle over that one, because Mom fixes everything with duct tape. Mentioning Mom and her crazy duct tape tricks also makes me think about next summer, when we'll be old enough to visit her house in North Dakota. Thinking about Mom and duct tape, I laugh even harder.

"What's so funny?" Brian asks.

"Talking about Mom and duct tape ... I was wondering if her whole house is held together with it!" Now we both double over with laughter.

Then I spy the simple toolbox nearby. I freeze. Mom's tools can't compare to the woodshop we use in Cub Scouts that has wall-to-wall tools, saws, and sanders. Yet there must be something we can build with all this lumber, even with just one hammer on hand.

Our campsite, Number 21 of the South Channel Campground, sits between Muskegon Lake, sand dunes, and thick woods. I catch sight of a giant oak tree growing in the campsite and notice its huge, chunky branches spreading out in every direction. Then it comes to me.

"We can build a ladder and climb that tree," I say, pointing to the tall oak. "We'll be able to spy on everyone." I crouch a bit and creep low, like a secret agent on a mission. Suddenly, I'm James Bond, the famous 007, in action. This is going to be ten times better than the Cub Scout one-board bookend or a single-tray bird feeder.

"That's a great idea! It'll be a secret hideout. The leaves will camouflage us," Brian says, stepping up to the tree to inspect its sturdy trunk and mass of leaves.

Next Brian begins to lay out the ladder formation on the ground. "Let's see ... we need to evenly space the short pieces for steps," my brother says, lost in thought like he's Professor Plum in the Library solving a murder. Uh, make that a math mystery.

"I'll grab the toolbox." I head to the camper with only a slight hitch in my step. The thrill of building has eased the discomfort of my swollen toe. I grab the one-and-only hammer and a box of mismatched nails. We'll make these tools work, I say to myself, while getting back to the construction project.

Already Brian has exactly measured the two long boards and placed each foot-long an equal distance from the one before it. My brother is long division in action.

While I hold the boards in place, Brian swings the hammer driving the nails into the wood. The ladder gets built lickety-split, and it boasts more rungs than the bunk bed ladder at home.

"Grab hold and let's raise it," I say, feeling excitement hum inside me.

Brian squats next to me and slips his hands under the ladder.

"One, two, three ... lift," I say. We pull with all our might, but the ladder barely moves. "Lift harder. We're almost under it." My face turns red as I struggle to get underneath the ladder. "Push up," I yell. My arms are high above my head now and start to burn from the weight they are bearing.

"Almost there!" Brian says, giving the ladder another shove.

"One more push!" I shout. "We're there. Let it drop!"

Timber! The ladder falls against the trunk of the tree with a loud thump. It leans rock-solid in place. With my brother's tiptop construction skills, he could be a superhero called Captain Hardhat maybe.

I leap in front and scoot up the solid masterpiece of two-by-fours, with Brian right behind me.

"We're up so high, the other campers look like Monopoly pieces," Brian says.

"And look, Red's outside shooting his slingshot."
I point to my friend, and then let out a little laugh

remembering how he got soaked by Hulk's supersonic water balloon during our target game.

I settle between two wide branches and sit to let my legs dangle. What an amazing secret hideout, hidden by all these leaves. For some strange reason, though, Brian is still climbing around to find a lookout spot. "You're wiggling the branches and making the leaves move," I say. "You're going to blow our cover."

"Hold on. I just need a level branch," he says. Brian's roaming causes twigs to snap and leaves to swish around worse than in a wind storm.

"Trees aren't exact. Just find a spot, will you!" I beg. But it's too late. I see Red turn his head toward the rustle of leaves and spot us up in the tree. He trots over and climbs the ladder, too.

"Hey, what are ya doing?" Red asks. Today he is without his T-ball cap. His mop of bright red hair plus glowing green eyes remind me of a bunch of Christmas M&M's.

"It's a secret hideout," I whisper, trying to sound like an undercover spy.

"Golly," he says, taking a wide-eyed look at me and then at Brian, who has now found his perfect spot hidden in the leaves. But Red doesn't stay put. He climbs back down and then climbs up again.

"Red! You need to sit still," I plead.

"Adam, he's only five. That'll never happen," Brian says.

Unfortunately, Red's ups and downs have drawn some more attention. A short kid with a chubby face and a funny mix of teeth – some big, some little – climbs up the tree. He bounces on a branch so fiercely it shakes with enough energy to power a city. His wild movement gets the attention of two more kids, maybe twins, because their lookalike faces are round as a can of beans. They climb on up and swing from branch to branch. In minutes, there's a boatload of kids in the tree.

So much for having a secret-hideout.

"Adam, we need more privacy," my brother says to me, folding his arms across his chest from his perch in the tree above me.

I shake my head and bite my lip, trying not to say "I told you so" about being noisy earlier.

"If we had more wood, I could build a tree house," Brian adds.

"Yeah, but we don't. And there's the other problem. We've only one hammer," I remind him.

I climb down, deciding there's more privacy on the ground, and then spot the rain tarp wrapped around our bikes near the back of the camper.

"Hey. I've got an idea," I call to Brian. "Come on down."

No response. Brian sits in the tree, gazing across the campground. He's in "the zone," thinking. He does this a lot. It must be all those math numbers rolling around in his brain.

Meanwhile, Red keeps going up and down the ladder like the EverReady rabbit. And the other kids? Now that all of them are up in the tree, they realize there is no one left to spy on down below. Bored, they climb out of the tree and move on. Even Red wanders away after a while, leaving only Brian up in the branches.

"Hey Brian," I call again. He still doesn't move. I let out a shrill whistle. The sharp sound snaps him out of his thoughts and he looks down. "Come here, I've got an idea."

While Brian scrambles out of the tree, I jog to the bikes and yank at the tarp. "This will make the perfect tent," I say, dragging it to the ladder.

Brian picks up the opposite side of the tarp. "Lift it up and over the ladder," he directs. "It's not quite even. Give your side a tug."

Just like that, we have a secret-hideout tent. We duck inside and see that it covers us completely. This is first-class. At least for a minute.

Whoosh! A wind gust whips by and a corner of the tarp flaps open, blowing our privacy.

"So much for your bright idea," my brother says. "This will never work without tent stakes."

Jeepers. We're living in a camper. There are no tent stakes! I take some deep breaths trying to stay calm and figure this out. "I'll just grab a few rocks," I say. It's a great plan, except that we're camping along sandy

Lake Michigan. Miles of dunes stretch everywhere, the result of glaciers grinding rocks into tons of sand thousands of years ago. Not only is the Muskegon State Park playground a giant sandbox, so is the entire West Michigan shoreline – no rocks here.

I crawl out of the tent and scout for choices. I find sticks to use as stakes, but how do I secure the sticks to the tent? There is no string in Mom's toolbox. Thread is too weak. Rope is too thick. Something in between is what's needed. Suddenly it comes to me: dental floss!

Dashing to the camper, I grab the floss from the bathroom. Back at the hideout, I wrap the tent corner around the tip of the stick and tightly wind the floss. Once secure, I push the stick into the ground. Bingo. The flap no longer snaps in the breeze.

With privacy back in place, I snatch two juice boxes from the cooler and take a minute to pull a Spiderman comic book out of my special cupboard inside the corner of the camper. Like a pirate's treasure chest, the cupboard is a private spot to hold my most valuable keepsakes. I bring the comic book and ice cold Blastin' Berry Cherry drinks into the wondrous hideout. From outside, I hear a twig crack and the sand squeaks from bare feet. We have company.

"Password!" I say, crawling through the opening of the tent.

"What?" It's Red, again.

"Password," I repeat. "You know. The secret word to gain entrance."

"Huh?"

"Have you ever been camping before?" I ask.

Red shakes his head no, eyes wide and round.

"Where are you from?"

"A big city far away," Red says.

"How far?"

"Longer than a school day," Red answers. After a few more questions, I learn that Red is from Chicago, where he lives on the 17th floor of an apartment building. "And the elevator moves so fast it feels like I left my stomach on the first floor," he says.

Unlike me, Red is an only child in his family. Now I understand why he doesn't know about passwords. When you have a brother, secret codes are a must. They're the only way to keep him out of your bedroom.

Red looks around for a clue, and he spies something on the far side of the campground.

"Is the password POND?" he asks. When he says "password," though, a funny little whistle floats out the space from his missing front teeth. The silly sound makes me giggle.

"Why do you think POND is the secret password?" I ask.

"Adam, have ya been to the pond?" Red asks.

"No, what pond?"

"Where the frogs are jumping," Red says.

"What frogs?" Brian asks as he climbs out of the tent. His curiosity is sparked by the idea of an adventure.

"The frogs over there," Red says while waving one arm in circles so I can't tell which direction "over there" is.

"Show us," I say to Red, snagging his flapping arm in an attempt to get him to focus. It works. Red turns and begins to march, grand marshal-style. He seems to be getting a kick out of leading us older boys. We pass the last campsite in the park and head toward an open field of waist-tall grass. The three of us stomp along a narrow path.

Up ahead, the path curves. Suddenly, there it is in front of us – the pond! It's smaller than a soccer field but, holy cow, more than a hundred frogs leap off lily pads in the center when we approach. Water ripples from their jumps and spread to the muddy edge where we stand.

It's exciting to think about being ankle-deep in muck again. I haven't caught a slimy frog since early spring at Dad's house. Back then, a sudden downpour of rain and tons of melting snow caused the small inlets of nearby Spring Lake to flood. Quickly, tadpoles and frogs were hopping out of water holes with every step we took. That is, until a heat wave in May dried up the swamps.

With toes at the edge of the pond, Brian scoops his hand across the water. "Darn, I can't reach the frogs."

"Here, grab my hand," I say, latching onto one of Brian's. "Try and stretch farther out."

"It's not working. I still can't reach them." Brian swishes at the water but it only sends the lily pads farther away.

"Red, do you know anyone with a boat?" I ask.

He shakes his head no. Dang it. Neither do I. Visions of stroking my first slimy frog fade away. No belly rubs. No croaks. No fun. All I can do is listen to their "rib-it, rib-it" teasing us from far away.

"Hey, wait. We don't need a boat," Brian says. "Let's build a raft out of the ladder."

What a brainstorm.

"We can float out and catch the frogs," I say. This is better than Huck Finn's adventure down the mighty Mississippi.

Eager to make the raft, we dash back to the campsite and rip the tarp off the ladder. I hustle under it and push, but it's really heavy. I lose my grip. The huge ladder swings out of control, gives me a mighty shove – and knocks me on my butt. The ladder hits the dirt with the power of a falling skyscraper yet, believe it or not, stays in one piece. My brother, Captain Hardhat, clearly builds 'em to last.

I gather the hammer and remaining nails while Red collects the extra foot-long pieces of wood. We're ready to start making the raft. Brian places a short board across the opening of the first step and whacks the nail in place. Red and I feed Brian board after board, working in a speedy rhythm like a racecar pit team. In a jiffy, the ladder is covered completely by wood.

"Get on the opposite end," I say. "We'll lift at the same time."

The raft doesn't budge. "Let's try again." We try to lift until our faces turn red and our arms sting from the effort. The ladder stays stuck in the sand.

"Don't worry. We can drag it to the pond," Brian says.

Wow. Another brainstorm. I quickly move to the end next to Brian and Red. The three of us squat and wedge our hands under the raft.

"Lift!" I grit my teeth. Our leverage raises one end. "Forward, march."

The raft is so heavy it carves deep ruts in the sand. One step at a time, we drag it down the smashed-grass path. Out of the corner of my eye, I see Freckles jumping through the tall weeds to chase butterflies. But the pond is in sight and our laser focus doesn't stray. My arms begin to feel like rubber from the dragging, but at last I see the frogs. Their green skin glistens in the sun.

"Let's raise it a little higher," I say as we yank on the raft.

Our arms are now high above our heads making us look like the spokes to a teepee.

"On the count of three, push it into the water," Brian says. "One, two - -"

Poosh! The raft hits the pond and sprays water everywhere. Instantly, my clothes are dripping wet and

I'm spitting cattail fuzz out of my mouth. It's a typhoon for the frogs, and they dive for cover.

And, as if it couldn't get any worse, I hear Red cry out, "The raft is sinking!"

"What? How come?" I ask.

"Uh-oh," Brian says. "The wood must be treated lumber."

"Huh? What's treated lumber?"

"You know, like wood used to build swing sets," Brian says. "It's covered in oily-stuff so the wood doesn't rot."

"And this means?"

"It also doesn't float," Brian explains. Oops. On second thought, maybe my brother isn't superhero Captain Hardhat.

I watch the raft sink to the bottom of the pond – and my heart goes down with the ship. It looks like I won't be feeling a frog's slimy belly, after all.

The enormous waves settle into small laps that touch my toes. Looking up, I spy a tree stump poking out of the water about two feet from shore. "Hey, I've got an idea. We can make the raft into a dock." I wade into the water.

"Adam, stop! Yer sinking!" Red yells.

"Nah, only a little bit. The bottom is soft and squishy," I say. "The pond isn't like the sandy bottom of Lake Michigan."

"Phew. What's that stinky smell?" Red asks as he wrinkles his nose. "It smells like dead worms."

"It's Adam," Brian says, holding back a laugh.

"Me? Why me?" I ask.

"When you stir up the murky water, it creates the stink," Brian explains.

"Does stinky mean it's good or bad?" Red asks.

"It's better than good," Brian says. "The rotten smell means this water brews bugs that frogs love to eat."

"Yeah, so let's catch some frogs," I say, ramming the end of the raft deeper into the muddy shore and lifting the other end onto the tree stump.

The raft is anchored tightly in place. I rub my hands together and once again dream about looking into the beady eyes of a slimy frog.

"Go ahead. Step on the dock," I say to Brian.

"No way. I'm the heaviest," he says.

"Yeah right. By barely five pounds," I say to my brother as I put my hands on my hips and lean toward him.

"No way." He takes a step closer to me. We're nose to nose and our eyes meet dead center. It's a stare-down between us. There's a hush across the pond. Even the birds stop singing. A moment passes.

"But you're older," I say.

Then a corner of Brian's mouth curls up. I see a sparkle in his eye. What is he thinking? Then it comes to me. I start to smile, too. Together, we turn and look at Red.

"Red, you're the brave one," I say, hoping Red buys the praise.

Red's eyes widen and his mouth goes round. He looks like a bowling ball. "You mean I can be first to catch a frog?" Red asks as he takes the bait and steps out. Hooray! The dock holds steady.

There's no need to wait any longer. I rush onto the dock, get on my knees, dip my hands into the water and reach for a frog. But these are pretty smart frogs. They swim toward the middle of the pond. Great. Just great. This is ruining my day.

"We need to reach farther out," Brain says.

"Who else do we know at the campground?" I ask.

"Adam, you're the kid that Dad calls a people magnet. You're always talking about a new friend at school. Even stray cats and dogs follow you home," Brian says. "Haven't you met anyone else at the campground?"

Hmm. Looking down, I remember my injured toe from when I tripped over the two-by-four. Wait! That was when Brian teased me about the girl I call Freckles. On the way to the pond, I saw her dancing in the grass catching butterflies. With a net! A net that could help us reach the frogs!

With a spring in my step, I'm off to search for Freckles and butterfly nets. She is not in the tall grass now. Reaching the park entrance, I see her, prim and proper in her crisp lavender dress with lacy socks and clean white sneakers. Doesn't she know the best part about camping is the dingy socks you get after wearing them for a few days in a row?

Freckles is sitting with two girls at her campsite picnic table. Three nets lay on the ground nearby. Since I don't have a sister, I don't know much about girls. Nor do I talk to them much. At school recess, I play catch with the boys. Luckily, I remember Freckles diving head first into the water balloon action. Gosh. Maybe she would like to trade her butterfly net for balloons.

I approach the girls, pushing down a nervous lump now in my throat. I can't believe what I will do to catch a frog.

"Would you like some balloons?" I ask as I lower my head and bat my eyelashes. My skin crawls doing such a silly movement, but I saw it work on TV. Quickly, I pull out red, blue, green, and yellow balloons from my pocket, hoping the sight of all the pretty colors will win them over. The girls' eyes grow large and I hear a quiet ooh and ah. I take this as a good sign.

But, Freckles folds her arms firmly, and I realize this is not a good sign. "Why are you being nice to us, Sweetie?" Freckles asks with a bit of a bite to her words.

I have learned it is best to tell it straight. Mom thinks I tell a lot of stories. I don't know why Mom doesn't believe me when I tell her a stray dog snatched the library book we can't find. So with Freckles, I keep it short and sweet. "I want to trade," I tell them.

43

She is curious now as her sea green eyes fix on the balloons. "Trade what, Sweetie?" Freckles asks. She calls everyone Sweetie, so this doesn't rattle me.

"Butterfly nets," I say, trying to sound like the nets aren't the most important thing in the world.

Freckles huddles with her girlfriends. They giggle. I don't know if giggling is a good sign. Then Freckles twirls her finger around one of her long, brown braided pigtails. What kind of sign is that? I wish I knew more about girls.

"Okay, Sweetie. We'll trade. We just finished trying to catch butterflies, but it's too hot. We'd rather cool off at the water spigot with water balloons," Freckles says.

I want to laugh out loud and confess my frog-catching motives, but I'm too smart to fail now. Instead, I toss over the balloons, snag the nets, and take off fast. My plan worked. And the best part is, I still have a secret stash of balloons in the camper.

With the nets safely in hand, I am back in the frog-catching business. Except for one problem. The weight of the frogs will pull at the delicate netting. Shucks, another snag. I have never worked so hard to catch a frog.

I rush back to the camper and search through the supply drawer. There must be something in here. I dig deeper and find Mom's secret weapon to fix anything – duct tape.

Hurrying back to Brian and Red, I holler, "I struck it rich!"

The boys see my haul, and their faces light up like shooting stars. Brian unrolls some tape and winds it around the rim of the nets. Then, he cleverly doubles it back over the handle, like a pro wrapping a boxer's gloves. Instantly the nets are sturdier and frog dipping-ready. Captain Hardhat strikes again.

We scoop for frogs all afternoon. I love stroking their bellies, listening to their croaks, and getting my fingers all pruney from the slimy and stinky muck. I could have stayed until dark, but Mom calls us for dinner.

After eating, the campfire is lit. I suck in the smoky air, listen to the wood crackle and watch the flames dance. I realize we never made it to the playground this morning to make new friends. But who would have thought leftover firewood and one magic hammer could outdo a Cub Scout woodshop filled with all the tools you would ever need?

Chapter 3

Goofy Makes Me Giggle

Like soldiers standing at attention, six little boxes are lined up in a row on the camper kitchen table. Delighted, I squeeze my eyes shut and cover them with my hands. "Quick, Brian. Name the six flavors of our mini-breakfast cereals before I do," I say. "Ready. Set. Go! Captain Crunch, Cocoa Crisp, Frosted Flakes - -"

But my oh-so-practical older brother interrupts me. "Quit playing games and pick one!"

I open my eyes. "How can I pick just one? Every box looks delicious!"

"If you don't choose first, I will."

"You can't! You picked yesterday. Now it's my turn."

This trading off-first dibs is one of those rare moments when I have the upper hand over my brother. He squirms in his seat and then drums his fingers on the table, waiting for my big decision. "It's just *cereal*," Brian says, making the word "cereal" sound stale and silly.

"No it's not," I snap. "We only get these cool little boxes when we go camping."

"But it's the same cereal we eat at home."

"No, at home, it's 'The Big Box Syndrome.' Morning after morning we eat the same thing until, finally, the whole box is gone," I explain. Doesn't he know that I dream about these special flavors all school year? I grab two mini boxes and make them march to the sound of a drum roll. "Bada-bum-bada-bing!"

"Adam, quit playing games. You're driving me crazy," Brian groans, leaning forward and banging his head on the table.

Mom calls from the back of the camper, "Have you finished your cereal yet? Grandma Barb will be here soon to go to the beach."

"Which beach?" Brian asks Mom while lifting his head off the table.

I cross my fingers. Our campsite, in the South Channel section of Muskegon State Park, sits between two lakes, and both lakes have beaches.

"The beach at Lake Michigan," Mom calls back.

Hooray! Today we are going to The Big Beach – the really great one. It is so big you can't see land across the lake. Water everywhere you look. And there's a snack bar with hot fudge sundaes and cotton candy. It's my favorite beach, hands-down!

The other beach, along Muskegon Lake, is really just fine but only a fraction of the size of The Big One.

But I wish Grandma was coming just a little bit later. It's ruining my chance to make Brian fidget and fuss for a change.

Mom steps up to the table and towers over me. With eyebrows up, she says, "I'll be outside packing for the beach, so Adam, pick your cereal." Her eyebrows may be brown as a chocolate bar, but there is nothing sweet about this look.

"Okay, okay," I say, giving up my moment of glory and choosing a cereal.

Brian quickly makes his choice, too, gulps it down, and dashes out the door to gather our beach gear.

My brother is always Mr. On Time. I, on the other hand, am just fine to have Brian do all the packing. I dillydally a little longer. Slowly, I fold back the cardboard flaps to the mini box and dribble in some milk. The cereal snaps. Mmm, I sniff in the fruity scent.

Then, as I open wide for the first yummy spoonful, my eyes spot Mom's cooking containers. Flour, oats, and rice stare at me from their clear plastic containers. One of these must be sugar, I think. Deciding to sneak a little more sweetness into the cereal, I flip off the lid and scoop out a mountain – or at least a big spoonful

– of sugar, and dump it in. One big swish with a spoon and then I take my first bite. Instantly, my mouth puckers and my eyes water. Gagging, I race to the trash and spit. Yuck!

None of the containers are labeled. For camping purposes, Mom packs small amounts from home. Cautiously, I dip my fingertip into the white mixture and put a tiny speck on my tongue. Just what I feared. It's salt! What have I done to my cereal?

"Yoo hoo. We're here!" I hear Grandma's voice through an open window in the camper.

"Adam. Get a move on!" Mom says her voice cutting through the window loud and clear.

My stomach growls from hunger, of course, but there is no time left to fix another mini box. My dream breakfast has turned into a nightmare. Quickly, I put the lid on the salt, shove it back with the stacked containers and whisk the cereal into the trash. While darting out the door, I snatch another snack for the beach.

"Hey, Grandma," I say, catching my breath and sneaking a handful of cheese puffs into the pocket of a beach tote.

"Sorry we're a tad late. I lost track of time reading this book. It's 'Friends Forever,' the latest story by Wanda Must," Grandma says, waving a hardcover book in the air. "I was on the library waiting list for three weeks until I got it. Now, in one day, I'm near the end."

"I had to tell her to finish the book here at the beach or she'd still be home reading," Papa says to all of us.

We call my grandfather Papa. It all started when Brian was a little kid. All he could say was *paah-paah* – and it stuck. Papa's last name is Schroeder. It's German, so when Papa says the "r," he always stretches it a bit, saying, "Schrrro-eder." He says the rolling of the "r" is proper English, but I think he means proper German. However, Papa is a big man and not someone I want to correct about grammar.

"Papa, are you taking a nap when we're at the beach?" I ask.

"Yes sir-ree. I deserve a rest after working forty-five years at Michigan Bell Telephone!" he says. Through a broad smile, he twirls the long ends of his silver-white mustache with two fingers. "These old legs have walked as many miles as Detrrro-it has telephone lines. And it's time to nap!"

Grandma is quick to correct Papa, "Alan, it's AT&T now. It hasn't been Michigan Bell for more than 20 years."

Papa shakes his head at Grandma's scolding. He shuffles off to the camper, adjusting his fedora. I have never seen Papa without his hat.

"Don't snore and scare the ants in my ant farm," I tease him, tipping my baseball cap. I am more like Papa than I thought. I don't go far without my cap, either.

"Don't worry, Adam, my snoring will sing your ants to sleep," he banters back.

Already dressed in swimsuits, Grandma, Mom, Brian, and I climb into the van and take the short ride to the beach. As we near the entrance, I hear the sound I have been waiting for this entire vacation – the roar of thunderous waves out on The Big Lake.

"Look at the huge rollers! The whitecaps are busting out, one right after another," I say. The waves come in fast and crash against the shore. It's not only loud, it's thrilling. I shift anxiously in my seat, nose pressed to the window.

"This is great! Usually, when we get powerful wind on Lake Michigan, it's stormy rainy weather," Brian says. "But not today! There isn't a cloud in the sky. I can't wait to hit the water and go bodysurfing."

"My heavens," Grandma says, "the lake is so big it reminds me of the ocean in Florida. But thank goodness it isn't. When I swim in that salty water, it stings my eyes."

Grandma doesn't know it, but after my salty breakfast, I'm glad Lake Michigan is fresh water, too!

Mom pulls the van into a parking space, and I hop out ready to ride the waves. Holy cow. The mighty wind snatches my Chicago Cubs baseball cap, but I catch it before it sails away. To keep it safe, I toss it back into the van.

"Everyone grab something to carry!" Mom calls out over the gusty winds. I snatch the folded beach blanket and dash ahead, knowing that laying the blanket is the first chore we have to do before we swim. While spreading out the blanket, the wild wind grabs hold of a corner and makes it fly up like a kite. Actually, more like a ship's sail. The blanket is as big in area as a queen-size bed. As it thrashes in the wind, it snaps like a whip. I squeeze the corner with a sturdy grip to hold on.

"Hurry! Bring that tote of beach toys over here," I call to Brian.

He hustles over. "Got it," he says as he snags a corner and anchors it with the tote.

"Put the cooler over there," I call out, pointing to the opposite corner of the blanket, which is soaring in the wind, too.

"This should secure it," Brian says, plopping the heavy cooler into place. Ice rattles when he sets it down. Next, he takes the woven picnic basket and puts it on the third corner. "That's all the beach gear," he says. Empty-handed, my brother darts away to start surfing the waves.

Cripes. I'm left holding onto the last corner until Grandma and Mom arrive.

"Grandma, can you sit here to hold down the blanket?"

"I can't right now. I forgot my book in the van and have to go back and get it."

"Mom, can you grab this corner?"

"No, Grandma forgot the van keys. I've got to catch up to her," Mom says, trotting off.

Jeepers. All I want to do is bodysurf, yet I can't leave. If I let go, the wind will snag the corner and the blanket will sail away, maybe knocking over the cooler and baskets, too. All I can do is stand here, watching the big rollers.

But, wait a minute. A shovel sticks out of the toy tote. I keep one foot on the last loose corner of the blanket and take a giant step across. Squatting, I reach out, stretching farther. I've almost got the shovel when the wind gusts and I lose my balance. Suddenly, I am spread eagle on the blanket. At the same time, the tote tumbles over and my cheese-puff snack spills. It takes just seconds for the hovering seagulls to swoop down, snatch the cheesy bits and sail off with my breakfast.

Worse yet, something plops on my head. A seagull scores a direct hit. "Darn sky-rats," I call out to the birds. Phew. A blob of bird poop smells worse than sulfur burning in science class.

So, here I am stranded on a blowing blanket, spread eagle, and stinking of bird poop. Plus, my cheese-puffs are gone. That's when I spy Freckles one blanket over. She's staring right at me, wearing a sparkly bathing suit with frilly stuff around the waist and a pink snorkel with matching pink facemask and flippers. Quite the contrast to my plain brown swim trunks.

"Tee-hee-hee," she starts, and then bursts out in laughter. Really, though, I can barely hear Freckles' laugh over the roar of the Big Lake wind and crash of the waves nearby, but with one hand she covers her mouth and her body jiggles with amusement. Instantly, my face feels hot. I'm certain it's bright red. Can I be lucky enough for her to think it's sunburn?

But a chance to swim in big waves doesn't come often. I decide I can't quit now. Inch by inch, I wiggle closer to the shovel. Finally, it's within reach. I roll back and scoop a mound of sand on top of the last corner. The wind whips but the corner stays put. At last, I can race to the giant swells and wash off this stinky gull smell.

I hit the water, and while running through the shallow waves, it's like I'm jumping hurdles. I lift my legs up to my chest and hop over each whitecap. Once I'm in knee-deep water, I plunge in and smash into a monster wave. Yeow! The cold water suddenly chills me, but I shake it off. I am focused on a mission. Fight the Big Surf.

Like Aquaman, my fourth-most-favorite superhero, I swim with super strength. My arms beat against the waves and my legs kick in the rumbling water. Before long, I reach the magic spot where water is up to my neck. Turning toward the shoreline, I look over my shoulder, watch, and wait. When the wave peaks, that's when I hop on for some bodysurfing fun. I sail along, nearly flying, at the tip of the wave. It's a long, glorious ride as the wave carries me at least twenty feet back to the shoreline.

I pop out of the wave into knee-high water and see Mom sunning on the beach. Not me, I'm ready to head out for another ride. With a surface dive, I plunge into the strong west wind and glide through the crashing waves. Nearby, Grandma Barb bobs in the water. She must have finished her book. Nothing stops Grandma when there's a new Wanda Must tale. I call her Wonder Mush because it seems every one of her stories that Grandma reads is about love and kissing. Ick.

Swimming out, I find Brian. We grab hands and hop on a wave. It's a crazy roller coaster ride for us, getting tossed high and low by the waves.

"This is awesome!" Brian and I cheer, slapping a high-five.

We swim out to catch another wave and pass Grandma Barb still bobbing in the same spot. Why do old people like to swim in one spot? Don't they know they're missing all the action?

Again and again, Brian and I ride the waves, getting whipped by the water. Sometimes we surf together and sometimes we fly alone. Hours later, with the sun low in the sky, it's time to load the van and head home. We're sunburned, pruney, and pooped.

On the short ride back to camp, I slip on my baseball cap. When the van pulls into the campsite, I smell smoke in the air and hear the crackle of a campfire. Unloading the van we notice Papa poking at the burning logs with his trusty fedora planted on his head.

"Papa, aren't you hot? It's eighty-five degrees and you have your hat on," Brian says.

"Yes sir-ree. This hat is part of my charm." Papa tips his hat.

"Not like Adam's hat," Brian says, elbowing me in the ribs. "There's no charm in a Chicago Cubs cap."

"Hey, you wanna bet! Alfonso Soriano almost touched it," I say to my brother, ready to fling my cap at him. But when I try to yank the cap off, it sticks to my sea-gull poop hair. Ouch, I mutter to myself. Well, at least Lake Michigan washed away the gross smell of bird gunk. Still, it will take a bucketful of shampoo to get the sticky poop completely out of my hair.

I change the subject quickly, because I don't want my brother to know I'm covered in bird doo-doo. "Hey, Brian, didn't you say you're getting roasting sticks to cook hot dogs?"

"Oh, yeah. I'm hungry after fighting the big surf." He wanders off to gather sticks. Good work, he's gone for now, and I can go shower after we eat. In the meantime, I'll keep the cap on my head.

Shortly, Brian returns with sticks. He sits down at the picnic table to carve pointed tips on them. Hmm. Four sticks: Papa, Grandma, Mom, Brian. I guess if I want to eat, I'd better go get my own stick. Across from the campsite, a sandy path leads into dense woods. It doesn't look well-traveled, but it looks thick with sticks and the hungry growl in my gut pushes me forward. Just my luck, though, a little way into the thick trees is all it takes for a swarm of black deerflies to find me.

How did I forget about these pesky things? Their favorite place is in thick woods, where the dense leaves shield them from the wind. And their favorite time of day to attack is near sunset, which is now!

Fiercely the deerflies bombard my head, fighting like tiny vampires for my blood. In seconds, they're biting me. I thrash my arms at the circling flies, yet the swatting does nothing to chase them off. I try to run, but trip, hitting the ground with a thump. The black cloud of bugs stays on me, drilling me. Ouch! More nasty stings. I flap at them with one hand and grab a pine branch with the other. Like a gallant knight, I thrust my pine-needle sword and swish it back and forth. Thank goodness it's enough movement to stop the flies from biting me, further. With my other hand, I snag a dead branch for a hot dog stick and dart away as fast as I can.

Once in the campsite clearing, the haze of wood smoke acts like bug repellent and the wicked deerflies retreat. I catch my breath and shake off the mishap. Shaking my head, I realize it was just this morning that I made another silly mistake. Something about breakfast cereal and salt.

Brian sits at the picnic table with four carved sticks at his side, all with sharp points waiting to spear their hot dogs. I can hear Mom, Grandma, and Papa rustling in the camper, probably preparing dinner.

Ready to carve my own stick, I pick up the knife from the table and start in on the wood. But shucks, there is a big knot in the stick right where the hot-dog point should go. I struggle to cut it away. Brian watches me and rolls his eyes. "Use the table," he says, tapping the picnic table with his hand.

"How do I do that?"

"Get the knot just at the edge of the table, face-up."

"Like this?" I say, putting my stick on the table and placing the knot so it looks me in the eye.

"Yes, it's all about leverage. Now, lean over, like this." Brian bends forward and puts pressure on a stick he has in his hand. Then, with his other hand, he extends his index finger, pretending it's a knife blade, and slides it along the top edge of the stick.

Clutching my stick in my left hand, I force my weight onto it and hold it steady. With my right, I thrust the blade across the bulging knot. In a snap, the stick is hot dog-ready. My brother's trick deserves a Boy Scout merit badge, but I just nod a thank you. I don't want him to think he's top dog.

"Are you ready to roast?" Grandma asks, coming from the camper with a tray of fresh hot dogs. "Everything else is set for dinner inside."

I settle onto the ground near the fire pit and begin roasting the dogs. "Hey, Grandma. Did you finish reading your book?" I ask, noticing she is relaxing in a lawn chair without the new book she was so eager to finish.

"Oh, Lordy. I'm not done reading it yet," she says.

"Didn't you finish the book at the beach?"

"Not quite."

That's strange. Ordinarily, Grandma loves her romance books. I shrug my shoulders. The sizzling hot dogs get my attention. They're getting juicy and plump. One more turn and we can munch the tasty treat.

During dinner, inside the camper, Grandma hands me a pink card with a raised gold flower in the corner. "Read the riddle, Adam," she says.

For years, Grandma has shared funny riddles with us boys. I can tell this one must be a really funny one, too, as I watch Grandma's face wrinkle into a wide grin and hear that familiar old clickity-clack noise. When Grandma laughs, her false teeth click. It's hard not to crack up at Grandma, but somehow I manage to read the riddle out loud with a straight face.

"I live above the ocean floor.

When swept by waves, I land on shore.

Pick me up, an echo roars.

What am I?"

I puzzle over Grandma's silly riddle. "A turtle would snap, not roar," I say, trying to work out the mystery.

"Coral lives in the sea, and it'd scratch if you picked it up. That would make me roar," Brian says. I shake my head knowing it's not the right answer, either.

Between bites of hot dog, Brian and I make guesses at Grandma's riddle. After each try, Grandma nods no. What can it be?

By now, I have the riddle memorized. With dinner finished, I leave the table to slip the pink card into my special camper cupboard. I flip the latch and open the drawer. Marbles roll about when I push comic books aside to place the pink card on top. I keep all my treasures in this drawer. With a light punch, the drawer clicks closed. The camper cupboards have special locks to keep stuff from spilling out when towing the camper down bumpy roads.

Heading outside with Brian, Mom, Papa, and Grandma, I unfold a lawn chair, sit back, and breathe in the cool evening air. I'm licking the last of the mustard off the corner of my mouth when Red strolls over from the campsite next door. Although Red is a lot younger, he has become a fun camping buddy. He has such a kooky, hiccup-like, little-kid's laugh. It makes me chuckle right along with him.

"I'm hungry," Red says.

"Go inside the camper to see if you can find a snack," I say, not wanting to move and feeling lazy after eating a yummy dog dinner.

Red hops up the two-step camper entrance. The screen door bangs behind him and then there's silence. He must be scouting the kitchen. Then I hear the screechy-scrape of the kitchen cupboard sliding open. I grin, knowing its strictly pots and pans in there. That door soon squeaks closed.

"Look at me!" Red calls out moments later. "It's soft and squishy!"

I watch his head appearing through the camper window. Now you see him, now you don't. I can tell he's bouncing and bouncing on the kitchen cushion.

"That's because it becomes a bed at night!" I call back to him.

Finally, he stops bouncing. Next, I hear a snap – the latch on a kitchen cupboard. It's quiet only for a second, then a familiar rattle – the sound of a stovetop popcorn tin.

"Can ya help me cook this Jiffy Pop?" Red asks Grandma as he pokes his head out of the small sliding window of the screen door next to the doorknob.

The window is big enough to hand out a juice box yet small enough to keep a whole swarm of bugs from invading the camper. It is not quite perfect for Red's head, though, and when he tries to pull his head back in, his ears get stuck in the frame.

"Help me, help me!" Red yells.

With every twist, his ears wiggle and his stuck head bobs like a jack-in-the-box. Red's silliness makes me laugh so hard I fall out of the lawn chair. Grandma goes to help Red get his head out of the opening, but this is too funny to miss, so I move closer to watch.

Years ago, when I was a little kid, I got my head stuck in that very same window. Grandma had to help me get unstuck, too.

Grandma gently presses her hands against Red's ears, flattening them to his head. Bending low, she softly says to Red, "Now, flash your handsome green eyes at the mosquito on my nose."

"What mosquito?" Red asks, quickly turning his head dead center, looking directly at Grandma's nose. Right at that very moment, when Red's head is straight up, not cocked and wiggly, Grandma pushes. Red's head pops out, he stumbles back, and I hear his butt thump on the camper floor.

"Are you all right?" Grandma asks, stepping into the camper to check on the boy. I follow behind.

Red lets out one of his kooky, hiccup-like laughs. Of course, this gets all of us all to roar. Between laughs, Red says, "Hey, there really wasn't a mosquito on yer nose, was there?" This gets us giggling more.

I extend my hand and Red latches on, pulling himself up off the floor. He snatches the corn package and gives it a shake. "Can we pop popcorn?" Red asks Grandma. The mouthwatering rattle of uncooked popcorn echoes inside the camper.

How can she say no? But Grandma doesn't say anything. She simply pulls open the apron drawer. Ever since Grandma was a cook at Southfield High School, she wears an apron when she cooks. Now she shares her special ones with us, keeping a supply in the camper.

"Golly, look at all those aprons," Red says, eyes bright.

"I have an apron for every season," Grandma says. "For Valentine's Day ..."

"A red heart!" Red beams and points to a red and pink apron.

"This one is for St. Patrick's Day." Grandma holds up another apron.

"A green flower?" Red asks, scratching his head.

"It's called an Irish shamrock," I say. "It's a lucky four-leaf clover. My favorite."

Red's excitement grows. He buries his head deep into the drawer and pulls out a fuzzy white headband. "Oh, look, rabbit ears for Easter."

"Absolutely, they match this yellow apron," Grandma says, unfolding an apron with bunnies and baby chicks.

Red gives the frilly Easter apron a quick glance and then dips his head back into the drawer. "Can I wear this white apron?" Red asks, picking out the snowman-shaped apron for his corn-popping duties. I giggle to myself. Just wait until he slips the apron over his head.

"Uh-oh. Frosty's carrot-nose touches the floor," Red says.

"Let's tie up the straps," Grandma says. "Okay, wiggle. There we go!"

I laugh a little more because Grandma had to tie my straps up when I was little, too. And just like me, Red has a big white bow on his butt.

Red and Grandma seem to have the popcorn project under control, so I fetch a Spider-Man comic from my treasure drawer and stretch out on the cushioned seat in the back of the camper.

"I'm ready to cook," Red says.

65

"Can you shake?" Grandma asks, squeezing the muscle on his skinny little arm.

"I'm the best. I'll be Chef Shaker," Red boasts.

But even on tiptoes he is too short to reach the stovetop. Grandma scoots the wooden toy box up to the stove, and Red hops up, becoming a foot taller. Next Grandma turns the knob. Whoosh, the gas flame lights. Red shakes the package across the open heat and the popcorn rattles. In less than a minute, Red says, "My arm feels like rubber."

"Use both hands," Grandma says.

Red wraps his other hand around the handle, too, and shakes so hard his entire body jiggles. The corn rattles – but no pops.

"Grandma, I think the package is supposed to get bigger," Red says.

"Well, goodness gracious, shake a little longer," Grandma encourages.

Red nods his head and shakes a bit more. But the corn is a rattling Mexican maraca. No pops. How unusual for Jiffy Pop.

Slowly, a faint trail of smoke drifts in the air. Followed by an unmistakable scent – burnt popcorn. This isn't good. Actually it's awful. Instantly, I'm off the couch. At the same time Brian rushes inside.

"What's going on?" he asks, waving his arms through the camper smoky haze.

Red stands on the toy box, still shaking the package. The big white bow wiggles on his butt. Brian and I hover over the little guy. It only takes a second to discover why the Jiffy Pop container hasn't expanded.

"Why is the cardboard still on the container?" Brian asks. "You have to take off the lid before cooking. Didn't you read the instructions?"

Grandma and Red stand with their mouths wide open. Red's eyes gaze up, water pooling in each corner. He blinks to hold on. "I'm too little to know how to read," Red says.

Brian and I look at Grandma. "Oh, dear. Well, I forgot to take my reading glasses off before I went swimming. The first giant wave washed them away. I can't read, either," she says, hanging her head.

My eyes catch sight of the salt container on the counter. Then at my deerfly bites. I break up laughing.

"What's so funny?" Brian asks.

I don't want to admit my silly mistakes, especially to my brother, so I just say, "It just goes to show, it doesn't matter how old we are, anyone can make a mistake."

"Yeah, and we can always learn from mistakes," Grandma says. "So let's cook another batch!" I reach in the cupboard and pull out another package of popcorn.

Chapter 4

Life Is Good When It's Crazy

Snip-snip. Snip-snip.

That's an odd noise. It's coming from out back, behind the camper. My curious nature gets the best of me and I trot back there to explore – and stop short. The picnic table is completely covered in long, narrow pieces of paper. Mom sits, snipping and trimming with scissors.

"What are you up to?" I ask.

"Oh, just getting started on an art project," Mom says.

"They look like paper swords," I say, picking up a long strip and swishing it in the air. But the skinny strip simply flops over.

"They're not swords, Adam." Her mouth tightens as she hides a little laugh.

Just then, something else catches my eye. It's Freckles pedaling by on a bike. Two braided pigtails trail behind, and on her head sits a glittery crown with stones that sparkle in the sun. Today she is wearing a yellow dress that looks like a piece of birthday cake covered in rainbow sprinkles. While Freckles prefers fancy, I'm happy in a plain T-shirt and tan shorts. It's like I'm whole wheat bread and Freckles is French toast smothered in butter with the entire spice rack shaken on top.

Freckles keeps on rolling, past our campsite, and follows the blacktop loop in the campground. I often see her whiz by on a bike, so I figure she'll peddle by again shortly.

When Mom shuffles the narrow paper bands, gathering them into a pile, the rustling sound draws my attention back to the table. After sorting them by color, Mom takes two red strips and one green strip, placing one strip over the other. Her fingers guide the strips back and forth, over and under. In seconds, Mom's weaving looks like Freckles' hair braids.

Just as I figured she would, Freckles pedals by again and I call out to her, "These papers look like your pigtails!"

Freckles circles back on her bike, but she doesn't slow down to look at the art project. In fact, it's just the opposite; she zips by me so closely that one of her pigtails whips across my face. Yikes. Freckle-cooties. And they're on my lips. Quickly I rub my hand across my mouth and try to wash my lips with spit. Maybe I need mouthwash. Or hand sanitizer.

Freckles circles again, this time much more slowly. As she passes, she flutters hello with her eyelashes at Mom, slightly tipping her head down so the crown thingy sparkles in the sunlight.

"Maybe your friend would like to join us, Adam?" Mom asks.

"No, no, that's okay." I touch my lips, still grossed out about Freckle-cooties.

"Isn't she the girl who gave you the butterfly nets to catch frogs?" Mom asks.

"Yeah, but I had to bribe her with my best water balloons."

"And who was the one who had hours of fun at the pond?"

"Well, the muck and slimy frogs were pretty cool," I say. In fact, her nets made it the best frog-catching day ever. Maybe I don't have Freckle cooties, after all.

Freckles approaches us again, still pedaling in slow motion.

"What pretty sequins on your dress," Mom says. "They match your rhinestone tiara."

Freckles stops her bike. "Yes, my tee-air-ahh." She drags out the word. That must be a fancy word for crown, I figure. "And my shoes match, too." She points a foot to show off her shiny sneaker. Doesn't Freckles know that, if you aren't in a T-shirt, shorts, and bare feet when camping, you're overdressed?

"Would you like to join us?" Mom asks.

Yikes! I give Mom a how-could-you look.

"Oh my, yes," Freckles says, her eyelashes fluttering again, now with excitement. "But maybe another time, I have to get home." She rides away, and I sigh in relief. I'm not sure I am ready to play with a girl.

With Freckles gone, my mind starts spinning as I watch Mom weave the red paper strips over and then under the green.

"So, why are you twisting paper like hair braids?" I ask.

"Yes, this weaving part is a bit like braiding." Mom's hands quickly flick the skinny strips over/under/over.

"And when I'm finished, it'll be called a collage, because I'll add other things to the paper."

Mom earns her living as an artist, painting pictures. It's interesting because she's always mixing things up. She'll glue tissue paper onto her paintings to make them bumpy like tree bark. Her art is rarely just paint on plain paper.

"Do you think you can you work magic with weaving like Grandma Barb works magic with cookies?" I ask.

Grandma puts a little flour, some eggs, and a heap of sugar into a big bowl. Then she adds oily stuff from a bottle, stirs it all up, and bakes it. Then, presto, we have yummy cookies. Right now, though, Mom's paper strips don't have the magical look of Grandma's cookies.

"Well, it's not magic, yet." Mom runs her hand over the plain red paper project. Even the bits of green aren't giving the art much zip. She looks up and gazes around the campground. Suddenly her blue eyes brighten, like a clear summer sky. "I could mix items from nature into the paper."

Using items from nature sounds a bit crazy. I nod my head, but not really in agreement. Secretly, I hope Mom doesn't sign our last name Moynihan to this art project.

Then Brian strolls up. "That's a lot of paper. What are you making?" he asks.

"I want to make a collage and weave items from nature in with these narrow strips," Mom says.

"Willow tree branches bend easily, and there's a big willow at the campground entrance," Brian suggests.

"That's a great idea. Let's get started," Mom says, her blue eyes now sparkling brighter than Freckles' crown. She leaves to grab some cutting tools from a supply box in the van.

"Okay, Hot Shot," I say to my brother.

"I didn't hear you speak up. Not even a hint of an idea. You just sat there like your lips were zippered shut." Brian snaps his mouth closed, and moves his hand across his lips to suggest they're sealed tight. "Mm ... mmmm ... mmm." He hums nonsense at me through his closed mouth.

The problem is my brother knows the right words to push my buttons. Like now, when he mocks me, I clench my teeth and squeeze my fists so tightly they shake. I've got more steam built up than Mom's pressure cooker on high heat. Dad says it's my Moynihan Irish blood. And somehow I got a double dose.

I take a stance, ready to lock horns with Brian. Then, lucky for my brother, Mom comes back.

"I know that look, Adam," she says, eyebrows raised knowingly. Then she lowers them and tries to distract me. "Have you solved Grandma Barb's riddle yet?" Mom knows wondering about the riddle will cool my hot temper.

"I think I'll work on solving Grandma's riddle down at the pond," I say. Besides, the croak of a slimy frog is ten times better than listening to Brian squawk. A boy's best friend is a dog, but I don't have one. So I figure telling all my troubles to a frog sounds like the next best thing for me.

"If you're going to the pond, remember the buddy system and take a friend," Mom says. "Come on, Brian, we'll go find that willow tree."

Before going to the pond, I stop next door at my pal, Red's campsite. No one is home, so I wander toward the playground, thinking it will be packed with kids so it'll be easy to find a buddy to bring to the pond. Parts of Grandma's riddle run through my head: *It lives in the ocean.* That means it likes water. Now I'm certain the pond will give me the answer to this challenge. I can't wait to be the first one to solve it! I race to the pond.

At the edge of the pond, my feet squish in the mud. The riddle says, "*When swept on shore an echo roars.*" I wonder if water snakes get swept on shore. The thought of giant snakes sends a shiver through me. Then I realize snakes don't roar and I don't see any snake holes. Just smooth, soft mud. I shake off the shudder and take a small step into the water. A cattail reed blows in the breeze and its brown fuzzy head brushes across my cheek. Green cattail reeds bend and curl like ribbon, reminding me of Mom's art project. Perhaps I can help, too.

I take a bigger step into the water to reach the cattail reeds. Instantly my feet sink into the mushy bottom, deeper than the day I waded in the water to save the drowning raft. This is strange. The glaciers that ground up and dumped a million truckloads of fine sand here thousands of years ago must have missed a spot.

Startled, I shift my weight. There's a squishing sound, and the black muck swallows me up to my kneecaps. In seconds, I'm thigh-high in mush. Could this be quicksand?

Deeper and deeper, it sucks me in. I tell myself I'm just a little excited. Not panicked. Not terrified. Just a little excited. Who am I kidding!? My heart pounds wildly against my chest. I should have a buddy with me, like Mom said, but I can't think about that right now. If I don't act quickly, I'll be eye-level with the frogs on the lily pads.

Grabbing the first thing in sight, I wrap both arms around a bundle of cattail reeds. They bend in my grasp as I sink deeper. The muck is about to reach my shorts. I'm going down fast. My weight forces the reed bundle to bend more than halfway.

Suddenly, as I'm pulling, the reeds fling me forward. I pop out of the muck and land on the ground, holding the yanked-out bunch of cattails.

It feels good to be out of danger, and my heartbeat settles down. But the smell. Phew! The black muck stinks worse than seagull poop. And I'm covered in it.

Luckily, by the time I drag the reeds back to the campsite, the black slimy coating on my skin has dried to gray and flaked away, along with most of the smell. As for the dried dirt on the hem of my shorts, that is pretty normal for me and camping life. I'm just glad Mom didn't catch me hip-hop dancing with the cattails without a buddy.

On the picnic table, the willow branches are piled high. And, sure enough, Brian is sitting there. Serious. Studious. Smart. He is just one year older than me, but sometimes it seems more like five.

Mom sits across from Brian. Hearing the rustle of cattails, Mom turns her head. "Oh, how wonderful. Isn't this great? Now we've got all kinds of choices. Come join us."

But I stay put.

"Adam, what's wrong?" she asks.

"Uh, I'm not sure I want to learn how to braid like Freckles' hair."

"This is weaving. It's different. Come on, join the fun," she says.

I shrug my shoulders. Oh well. There isn't much else to do, so I settle in on the bench next to Brian. I pick purple strips. Then, on second thought, I change my mind and grab yellow, orange, green and every other color I can find. Whatever I end up with, at least it will be lively.

"Over, under, and through." Mom starts the weaving lesson.

My hands thread the skinny bands of paper. Here and there, I mix in cattail reeds, pushing them in and out the other side.

Glancing at Brian, I notice he isn't weaving. Instead, he sorts his strips into two piles. Exact piles of only red and blue. He has such a different approach than me.

"I'm weaving the blue strips across and threading the red from top to bottom," Brian explains. His style forms a perfect checkerboard. It is straight, sturdy ... and boring. That is, unless we had checkerboard pieces and could play a game on it.

Then, I look down at my weaving. It's colorful, but flat as a pancake and seems even less exciting than Brian's checkerboard. Boy, does my paper pancake need something extra, like a river of maple syrup or perhaps a mountain of whip cream. But, my art project isn't food. I wonder what I can do to jazz up paper and reeds.

Uncertain, I start to tug one of the strips. It starts to curl as the weaving is pulled tighter. Suddenly I have an idea. "Hold here," I say to Brian, pointing to a corner.

"What for?" he asks, eyes fixed on his even-steven checkerboard.

"I'm trying something different. I need your strong arms." My fake praise gets Brian to lend me a hand. Yanking harder, the pancake begins to curl. Something magical is happening! I pull again, harder this time. It's a tug-of-war – except it's with reeds.

"Why are you pulling so hard?" Brian asks, unable to figure out my idea.

"Just keep holding, Brian. And be patient." I grin to myself, because my brother is usually the patient one. Against the table leg, I brace my foot for leverage. This forces more tension on the reeds, and the woven pancake curls into a basket shape. My plan is working.

"Hey, Adam, it looks like a bowl," Brian says as he starts to figure out my plan.

"Don't let go." I step aside, leaving Brian to hold the bowl steady. From the pile of left over reeds on the ground, I select three soft ones and flick one strand over the other. "Almost done. I'll be back in a second."

My hands flip and twist the three reeds. In a flash, I am braiding a rope that copies Freckles' braids. I never thought I'd be inspired by a girl, especially one who looks like she's ready to walk down a fashion runway even when she's camping.

"What's that?" Brian asks, as he studies the braided rope with a wrinkled brow.

"A handle to make a basket." I step up to the bowl and tie the ends of the rope to each side.

"Wow! It looks like an Easter basket," Brian says. "Hey Mom, can we have a Crazy Day?"

This time my brother's words don't push my lock-horn button – they push my whoop-and-holler button. Crazy Days are something Mom started doing with us years ago because Brian and I spend many of the exact days of a holiday with Dad. So with Mom, we celebrate holidays on a different day than the calendar tells us. What kid doesn't like to celebrate things more than once?

"Leave a note for the Easter Bunny and see what happens," Mom says, her voice sounding sly as well as sneaky. Her blue eyes flash a look as mysterious as the bottom of the ocean. Yet I have a feeling she might be up for a Crazy Day in August. This project could top Grandma's cookies, except for the writing to the Easter Bunny part. That feels like homework.

"I know what I'll write," Brian says, hopping into the camper to get a head start. I'm left behind.

My stomach tightens at the thought of penmanship. Yet, to get some jelly beans out of this, I force myself to buckle down. Setting up back at the picnic table, I snatch the paper pad Papa uses for crossword puzzle notes and flip to a blank page ready to start. "Let's see - -"

"I'm done," Brian says while flying out of the camper and waving a sealed note in an envelope.

I plop my head down on the picnic table.

Mom steps over to me, takes my hand, and gives it three short squeezes. That's Mom code for I love you.

"Adam, why not draw a picture?"

That's just the right idea. Without hesitation, I draw swirls with my pencil, knowing Mom will think it's a fluffy bunny. After adding two eyes and a dot for the nose, I am ready to lick an envelope and seal my Crazy Day note, too. My brother may have finished before me, but I got the job done in another way.

That night, while sleeping, I dream of foil-wrapped chocolate, marshmallow candy, and jellybeans.

I wake up early, even before the birds are singing. A narrow strip of orange morning light shines through the camper window. It's enough daylight for me to race to the window and see the Easter basket on the picnic table, spilling over with candy! My mouth waters as I tiptoe outside.

Brian wakes up soon after, and the morning is spent sorting and counting candy. But mostly, I eat it.

Before I know it, lunch is ready. Mom carries out sandwiches, fruit, chips, and milk to the picnic table on a tray. "When you're done, we'll drive to town for supplies." With that, she returns to the camper.

"Your face is green," Brian says to me.

"Yours would be too if you ate as much candy as I have."

"Well, eat your sandwich anyway, I want to go to the store to buy a new Play Ball DVD," Brian says. My brother loves to learn and study baseball strategy. He has already read every Matt Christopher book about baseball.

I look at my sandwich. It's so big it covers the entire plate. Maybe if I take a deep breath. Nope. That doesn't help. I fall sideways onto the picnic bench, groaning and holding my stomach. "Will you eat my sandwich?" I ask Brian.

"No way, I already ate mine," my brother says. "And hurry up. If you poke around much longer, the store will be closed." Brian takes his empty plate into the camper.

How can candy taste so good one minute, and the next minute make you feel sick? Moaning, I roll myself into a sitting position. Suddenly, two furry brown animals scurry across the sandy campsite and slip under the thick bushes. Squeaky chatter fills the air. My face breaks into a smile. The sandwich no longer looks so big.

Quietly, I creep to the edge of the campsite, break the sandwich into little pieces and whisper, "Here you go little fellows." On tiptoes, I sneak away. In seconds, the chipmunks scamper over, snatch the scraps and take away my too much lunch. I carry the empty tray into the camper.

Minutes later we're riding along Memorial Drive. We hit the first stop sign at Wild Wood Marine. That's when I spot it. "There's one," I say. My pulse quickens.

"Wait, there's another. And it's bigger," Brian says.

I lean over as far as I can to Brian's side of the van, but I can't see his. "Which one do you think is biggest?" I ask.

"Hold on, there's one more," Brian says.

"Mom, can you please slow down?" I beg.

Only twice a year do these tents pop up, before the Fourth of July and now, when Labor Day is near. For sale in those tents are hundreds – thousands – of fireworks. I save all my money during the summer just for a chance to shop in these tents.

"Do we get two stops this time?" I ask Mom. It will break my heart if she says only one.

"Two stops," she says. Those words are music to my ears. "It's a two-tent limit," she adds. "Otherwise, it'd take all day." Mom is a grown-up. She doesn't realize firecrackers make the greatest show on Earth.

"Let's do the yellow tent first and then the blue one," Brian says.

I try to answer but nothing comes out. The excitement has stolen my voice. All I can do is nod. Thank goodness Brian is thinking clearly.

The van stops. I rush to the yellow tent and spot hundreds of Black Cat firecrackers. Next are aisles of bottle rockets, and then row after row of snakes. Along the back wall are tables of cherry bombs. I've saved ten dollars for this. That's more money than I get from Grandma on my birthday.

"Over here, Adam," Brian says. "Look at these!" He rolls a cylinder shape in his hand. "It's a Roman candle."

"Should we get it?" I ask, but then hesitate. "How much does it cost?" I'm trying to add prices in my head, but I lose count every time I spot a different firecracker. With so many choices, I have to pick carefully.

"Ladyfingers, whistlers, and army tanks are over here!" Brian calls out to me.

Scanning all the choices, my head spins. This is way better than a toy store.

"Remember we need to get as many fireworks as we can for our money," I say. "That way, we can shoot them off the entire night."

I run from table to table. Ten boxes of snakes for twenty-five cents per box, plus the cost of a Roman candle. I also want some bottle rockets for fifty cents apiece. In school, I'm good at math. But, here in the tents, I'm too excited to keep numbers straight.

"Are you getting smoke bombs?" Brian asks. "We need to make sure we don't get the same things."

"Let's put our pile of fireworks and our money together," I say. This will make things easier. I'll let my older brother add the prices. Brian is always exact. Besides, I want to focus on choosing firecrackers.

We collect the best fireworks our twenty dollars can buy. Leaving the tent, we each carry a bag so big, our arms can barely hold on. Now comes the tough part, waiting for dusk to shoot them off.

When we return from town, I help unload groceries and then sweep the camper floor. Brian and I sort the fireworks, twice. I sit outside and drum my fingers on the picnic table. The clock ticks, but the minute hand seems stuck in the same spot. Not even the Easter basket helps pass the time, and Brian has his nose buried in the baseball book that came with the DVD he bought in town.

"Mom, do you think it's dark enough yet?" I ask as soon as she steps out the camper door. It's the third time I've asked. This time I hope the answer is yes.

"Gather your things and we'll review the safety rules," Mom says.

I jump up, grab the fireworks, and snag some matches from next to the camper stove. I'm back at the picnic table in less than a minute. Brian is ready, too.

Mom is big into safety. Each year, we get to help a little more with the lighting of fireworks. I can't wait for the day I'll be old enough to do it all by myself.

"I think the pond is the safest place," Mom says. "No one is around, and the hot fireworks will land in the water. That way we don't start a fire."

At times like these, I call Mom, Mrs. Safety. Of course after sinking in the muck at the pond earlier today, I'm glad she reminds us to be safe.

"We'll need one more tool," Mom says, and she heads back to the camper.

I put the fireworks into one giant pile on the picnic table and then notice the idle Easter basket and pick it up. The braided handle is strong and secure. This would be perfect for carrying the fireworks. I dump out the few remaining pieces of candy and fill it with the treasured firecrackers.

Swinging the basket, I wander in a circle and wait for Mom. I wonder what's taking so long in the camper. Trying to be patient, I walk in a circle again, only this time backwards, so it takes longer. Finally, the screen door clangs. I look up, and there stands Mom with another bag just like the big ones we got at the fireworks tent.

"You're old enough to shoot more firecrackers this year. I bought a few extra," she says.

For a girl, Mom sure has some great ideas. Like thinking fireworks are the best things in the world after all!

Chapter 5

Trapped in a House of Beauty

For three days now, I've been stuck in a tin box with the rat-a-tat-tat of rain drumming over my head. I wonder if I'll ever escape this camper.

"Adam, do you want to play Old Maid?" Brian asks.

"Nah, we've already played a thousand times," I grumble and squirm.

"Hangman?"

"No."

"I – Spy?"

"I've spotted everything red, blue, or green," I sigh. "I don't want to spy anymore." I pace the narrow aisle. Turning, I take the same six steps back. When I hit the end of the camper, I catch sight of a small gold plaque stuck in the corner. Leaning forward to get a closer look, I read it aloud, "Terry Taurus Travel Trailer, 18 feet, weight 3,500 pounds, sleeping capacity 6." Humph. I pace back. "How would you squeeze six people into this camper? I think three is too many," I snarl.

Brian is quick to comment. "I know, Adam, you've been bumping into Mom and me every time you walk by." His legs hang out into the aisle as he sits on the kitchen bench seat and shuffles cards for his next hand of solitaire.

"It's just that I feel like Meijer, stuck in a cage," I say. Meijer is my furry guinea pig at Dad's house. Unlike me, though, Meijer likes to burrow himself into a corner, hunker down and stay put for hours.

Ping, ping, ping. The rain pecks at the tin ceiling. Jeepers. Until now, I've always loved camping, but with this rain, it's boredom in a box.

In the distance, I hear the ghostly groan of the foghorn off Lake Michigan. Baa-room, the horn blares rhythmically every two minutes. Each time, its long eerie wail sends a cold shiver through me.

"Do you think that horn will ever stop?" I ask Brian.

"When the storm ends," he says. "The lighthouse foghorn is made to warn boaters."

"Yeah, I know that," I mutter to myself.

Mom gets out the small travel bag she carries camping. It's pink, with frilly flowers, and it's filled with beauty products.

I pace by and see Mom brushing her teeth at the sink. On the counter, the unzipped bag gushes with bottles in every shape and size. I get a whiff of something smelly, yet sweet, like Grandma's rose garden perfume. Stepping up to the counter, I sneak a peek inside the bag. Mom's travel bag is like the teacher's lounge at school – you never know what really goes on in there.

"What's this?" I point to a long, skinny tube, uncertain if I should touch it.

"It's cream for your face," Mom casually explains as she puts away her toothbrush.

The familiarity of the toothbrush gives me courage to tap the tip of a metal gadget that pokes out. "This looks like a Swiss Army knife," I say.

"It's simply a toenail clipper. Not nearly as deadly, har, har," Mom snickers with one eyebrow arched, like a pirate. I can tell she is trying to humor me, hoping to chase away the rainy day blues.

A blast of wind rocks the camper and hisses through a crack where the door doesn't shut tightly. The rain continues to drum on the metal roof above our heads. The travel bag seems to be the only escape from my archenemy, boredom.

Taking a chance, I grab a bottle. Clear gel slowly oozes down the side. "And this is?" I ask.

"Facial toner," Mom says.

I can't believe I'm asking about this girl stuff. My sensible side is telling me to turn and flee, but the bored side is telling me to dive in and take the dare. "Can I try it?"

"Sure." Mom's brown eyebrows lift with excitement. Their melt-in-your-mouth chocolate color makes me relax a little.

So I sit down and that's when my stomach tightens. "Is this beauty stuff safe for a kid?" I ask.

"Well, I've been using this make-up routine since before you were born," Mom says with a hint of a soft ha, ha, har. It's that special laugh that tells me she's on my side.

"Then, I guess it's okay." I shrug my shoulders.

The wet cotton swab softly moves across my face. Mom's gentle touch sweeps along my forehead, down my nose and across my chin. It relaxes me, putting me in a trance. Suddenly, there's a burning feeling.

"It's getting colder. And itchy." I squirm in my seat, getting a bit nervous.

"Oh, that feeling is the gel tightening your skin. That's why it's called toner," Mom says.

But the burning sensation grows stronger. I start to wonder if this is nuclear waste on my face. I bite my lip, fearing my skin might turn into crusty moon craters. But then the sting slowly turns gentle and cool.

I glance back at the pink bag. Then I look at Brian, now consumed in reading. Since there aren't many choices, I decide to take another chance on girl stuff.

"Um, Mom, I'll try something else," I say.

"Great! Let's style your hair. We'll put some gel in it."
Mom pulls out a tube of hair gunk and squeezes a glob of
it into my hand.

"It looks like Grandma's wallpaper paste," I say.

"Not hardly," Mom says. "Now, rub it between your
hands and then swish it through your hair."

The goop squishes between my fingers. I plop it
on top of my head and slide it through my blond hair.
Instantly, it stands straight up.

Mom starts to giggle. Her laugh is loud enough to get
Brian to look up while drinking a soda. One glance at me
and pop spurts out of his nose.

"You look like you were zapped by lightning," Brian
says between hiccups and laughs.

"Ha-ha," I grumble, yet I wonder what Mom has done.

"Spread the gel around a little more," Mom advises,
struggling to keep a straight face.

"I think you gave me the long-hair dose." My eyes are
glued on Mom's brown, shoulder-length hair. My hair is
cut short, about one-inch, tops.

"Oh, maybe so," Mom says. Now she bites her lip in
an effort to hold back laughter. I roll my eyes at her.

"Don't worry, Adam, I'm sure it will wash out," Brian
says. The girl stuff craziness draws Brian in, too.

He wanders over, snoops close to the bag and takes
a sniff. For Brian to step outside the box and try a
product that says "girl" and not "boy" is more daring than

jumping the Grand Canyon on a motorcycle. The beast of boredom breaks even my brother.

But Brian plays it safe, only looking not touching. "Facial mask," Brian reads aloud on a bottle label, but he is careful not to touch it. His green eyes spin with curiosity, or maybe fear. I can't tell which. "Should I try some, Adam?" he asks.

I pat my hair. My hand bounces off. Maybe I should warn him, but I decide to let him take a chance on Mom's wisdom.

"What if Lucas finds out?" Brian is quick to remind me of my best friend back home. We nicknamed him The Rhymer.

"Uh-oh, I forgot about Lucas. Do you really think he could make up a rhyme about girl stuff?" I ask.

"Brian Moynihan, he's a beauty fan, keeping his face spic-and-span," Brian rattles off.

"How did you do that so fast?" I ask, thinking only Lucas could whip up rhymes so quickly about our Irish name.

"Rhyming isn't difficult. The problem is Lucas. He sings rhymes – everywhere!" Brian says.

"Well, I won't tell if you don't tell," I say. My brother is as honest as Abe Lincoln. He will keep the girl stuff secret.

Brian swallows hard and then lets Mom spread thick, creamy facial mask onto his face. He looks like a giant cookie covered in a layer of pink frosting. I wish I had candy sprinkles to throw on his pink face.

But Mom catches the gleam in my eyes and quickly sends Brian to the bathroom to wash off the drying mask.

On his way, Brian struggles to speak around the hard and crusty beauty mask. "My flace pleels like it'll bleak."

Laughing, I decode his message. "My face feels like it'll break."

"Okay, Adam," Mom says. "Let's do your eyebrows next."

I turn toward the snapping sound of tweezers that look like mini pliers. Hmm. What the heck, I think. Mom pinches the tweezers to my brow and pulls. An instant blast of pain shoots between my eyes. "Ouch! I'm a plucked chicken." I rub the spot of the yanked-out eyebrow to ease the prickling feeling. "Girl stuff is miserable. Just like this rain. It must be Lake Effect Rain," I gripe.

"You're getting that mixed up with Lake Effect Snow. That happens in the winter when moisture brews across Lake Michigan," Brian explains, referring to the weird weather that happens near The Big Lake shoreline. Brian is patting himself dry with a towel. He no longer looks like a face made of pink cotton candy.

"Well, maybe so," I say about his weather explanation, "but this is just like Lake Effect Snow. There's no sun, only dark skies and tons of wet stuff for days on end."

"Adam, call it what you want, but it's still keeping us inside, isn't it?" Brian says.

"Yeah, it sure is." I slump onto the kitchen bench.

"Let's do a pedicure," Mom says.

"A what?" I ask.

"Pedicure. A fancy word for foot care," Brian says.

Another crazy beauty plan. On the flip side, well, I guess there isn't a flip side or any better choice. So, I let Mom stuff cotton balls between each of my toes.

"Look, I'm a penguin in a beauty shop." I stand up and try to take a step.

Brian unscrews the bottle cap of hot pink nail polish and then yanks out the brush. "Are you ready for this?" He plunges the brush back into the bottle and then charges with it toward my toes.

"No! Wait! Wait! I'm not that bored," I beg and jerk away from his reach.

The cotton balls soar through the air. Brian swings at the floating cotton, hits it, and it whizzes inches from my head. The cotton-ball attack is on. With a fistful of cotton, I pounce on Brian and tickle his face. It's great to be doing boy stuff again.

Acting silly, I take a wad of cotton balls and place them above my upper lip. "Look, it's Papa's mustache," I say.

"No, like this," Brian says, rolling the cotton ball on the table, back and forth, like making a Play-Doh snake. But when Brian holds it up to his face, the thin cotton strip just droops.

"Here, use this." I grab the hair goop, squeeze out a blob, and work it into the cotton.

"Great idea. It's as sturdy as Papa's mustache wax," Brian says. He snatches the cotton snake and curls the tips. The curled snake holds firm. It's as stiff as my Frankenstein-looking hair.

"What if this hair goop really is mustache wax?" I suck in some air as panic runs through me.

"Breathe, Adam, breathe," Brian says as he pats me on the back. My brother knows that sometimes I forget to breathe when I'm upset.

My breathing calms and my heart quiets. I squeak out another question, "Do you think school will be starting by the time I get this stuff out of my hair?"

"Don't worry," Brian says. "If you add a little campfire smoke to that hair, you won't have to worry about girls chasing you."

I don't know if this is a good thing or not. I look at Mom.

"It'll wash out," she says. But with no loving laugh. No har, har, har, like her silly pirate imitation. Is she on my side? My heart races again.

Ping-pa-ping-ping. The heavy rain keeps beating against the tin roof. I realize with this endless rain, I don't have much to worry about. What does it matter if I have stiff hair when I'm stuck inside a camper?

Luckily, Mom makes up a game to keep us busy for the rest of the soggy, wet evening. This time, no girl stuff. Instead, it's a guessing game. With her finger, she gently draws imaginary letters on our backs. We can't see her hand. We can only feel her tender touch as she outlines the shape. It's easy to guess each letter one at a time, but she makes it tricky.

"M ... a ... d," I guess. Wait, there is more as I feel her soft touch again. "A." It's a word scramble, too. I think it through and it comes to me. "The answer is Adam!" I shout.

We have fun guessing and taking turns. Soon, it's bedtime. We brush our teeth with ordinary toothpaste, not a fancy girl flavor, like peppermint stripe with whitening beads, and I couldn't be happier. We unfold the beds and hit the sack.

Waking up the next morning, I realize the camper roof is dead silent for a change. No pecking and pinging and rat-a-tat-tatting. Which means no more rain!

I fly out of bed, whip on shorts, a shirt, my baseball cap, and flee the camper.

But outside, I have a rude awakening. With every step, my shoes squish in the mud. Huge puddles are everywhere. It is too wet for baseball. And the wind is so strong; it stirs up waves too big to swim. Even Red isn't playing outside. Muskegon State Park is like a ghost town after days of rain.

Fighting a blast of cold air, I shiver and shove my hands into my pockets. It's wetter and soggier outside than breakfast cereal left floating in milk.

A gust of wind whips the ball cap off my head. My Frankenstein hair stays put. I chase after my hat as it sails into a clump of weeds, then snatch it up, and slap it back onto my head. Rotten weather ... rotten campground ... rotten vacation! Then I hear a groan.

It's Mom, at the back of the van, with rope piled around her ankles. "Hey, Mom, what are you doing?"

"Just trying to get all this rope unstuck." She gives it a mighty tug. Oops. It loosens and she plops on her butt, just missing a big puddle. Only Mom.

"Here, let me help you up." I jog over to offer a hand.

"I thought we could play jump rope."

"Please, please, no more girl stuff," I beg.

97

"Jump rope isn't just for girls," Mom says.

I give her an are-you-out-of-your-mind look.

"Professional boxers jump rope." she says with a hint of that special ha, ha, har laugh that comforts me. Come to think about it, I have watched prizefighters on TV jump rope so quickly you can't even see the rope going round. Fact is, I'm a fast runner, so maybe I can jump rope, too.

"Help me tie this," Mom says as she moves ahead and wraps one end of the rope around a tree.

I give Mom credit for trying to think of something fun we can play in a campground full of puddles. She's a roll-with-the punches kind of person. I wander over to the rope and tie my best Cub Scout square knot.

The knot holds tight, so Mom grabs the other end and gives it a twirl.

Beep, beep. A car horn toots. Papa and Grandma pull up to the campsite in their truck.

"Hey, Grandma, Papa, we're playing jump rope," I sing out to them, across the campsite.

"I used to be able to jump rope," Grandma says as she gets out of the truck and heads straight for us.

Papa tips his fedora at me and then shakes his head at Grandma. "I'll let Grandma be the one to jump rope with you," he says. "It's time for my nap." Grandpa shuffles into the camper.

"New eyeglasses, Grandma?" I ask, knowing she lost her last pair swimming in the giant waves.

"What? I can't hear you," she says. Oh boy. Grandma can't see, she can't hear, but she thinks she can jump rope. She marches up to the twirling rope and nods her head to the click as it taps the wet sand. Her new glasses slip down her nose, but she is too busy watching the rhythm to push them back up.

She enters the rope. Jump, jump, jump. Her style is a bit like a peg-leg pirate. It must be from her knee surgery last year. But look at her go! Jump, jump, jump! I cover my mouth to try not to laugh out loud.

If Grandma can do it, I guess I can, too. The rope circles once around, I take a chance, and dart in. Shoop. Swish. My moves are Ninja quick. Dust would fly if it hadn't just rained.

By this time, Brian is out of the camper and ready to join in. He watches the rope spin. And watches. And watches.

"When the rope is at the top, just run underneath it," I say.

"Don't worry, I will. Just give me a minute."

The rope goes 'round, and 'round, and 'round. My brother tends to be cautious. Finally, he enters, taking long, steady, single jumps.

"Let's play one of those singing games," I say.

"I don't know any jump rope songs," Brian says.

"Me neither," Mom says.

Grandma starts laughing, "That's a good thing. When your Mom sings in the shower she squeals like a guinea pig." Grandma screeches and twitches her nose when she says, "squeal." Even Mom laughs at this.

"Singing off-key must run in the family then," Brian says with a smirk. "I don't think any of us are good singers."

"Hey, Adam, I have an idea," Mom says. "Your friend, Freckles, she'd know jump rope songs."

"Maybe," I say. "But I haven't seen her outside today." This is probably just as well. What if she were to beat me at jump rope?

"Wait a minute. I used to know some songs." Grandma runs a hand through her gray hair. Her glasses still sit low on her nose. "Woe is me. Wait, I remember a game. It's called School."

Whew. That means Freckles won't be playing jump rope.

Grandma explains the game. "Kindergarten is running through the rope. No jumping. First grade, enter and jump once, and then get out. Second grade is two jumps. We'll play up to high school."

This seems simple. I have already jumped thirty-nine times in a row. If we had a trophy, I am sure I'd take it home. Boys are good at jump rope.

We start the game and quickly zip past grades K through four.

"I'm stuck on fifth grade," Grandma says as she trips in the twirling rope.

My turn is next.

"Is that your third time trying to pass sixth grade?" Brian asks.

I nod, but to the rhythm of the rope rather than answering my brother. "This is harder than it looks," I say, trying to get into the rope at just the right time.

The game moves on. Grandma takes the lead. I guess it doesn't matter that she can't hear or see.

Eleventh grade gives me trouble. It's getting close to the end of the game. I tap my foot anxiously for my next chance. But Brian's turn is before mine. He jumps flawlessly, soars ahead, and wins. Now I'm glad there isn't a trophy. Oh well. At least a boy wins this girl's game.

"So, have you boys solved the riddle?" Grandma asks as we all sit down for a break.

"No. I know it's something that lives in salt water," Brian says. "But I'm stuck on the roar."

"And the echo puzzles me," I say.

Grandma reaches out her hand and pretends to hold something in her palm. Slowly she closes her fingers around an imaginary object. Then she puts her cupped hand up to her ear. "Listen," she says almost in a whisper.

"It's a seashell! The kind you can hear the ocean inside!" I yell.

At the same time, Brian shouts, "Conch shell, conch shell, conch shell!"

From her jacket pocket Grandma takes out two conch shells. We hold them up to our ears and there it is – the ocean roar.

"I brought them all the way from Florida for you boys." Grandma cuddles Brian and me into her arms. A hug from Grandma is like hugging a pillow. A big soft pillow that smells like a rose garden.

I take my seashell and slip it into my special cupboard in the corner of the camper. I feel a quick and pleasant flutter in my heart when the cupboard snaps shut.

Grandma and Papa head home. It's late afternoon by now, and finally the sun shines brightly and the wind settles into a light breeze. Most of the puddles are even gone.

"Where are you off to, Adam?" Mom asks as she sees me hop on my bike.

"To catch a few slimy frogs," I say.

"No more girl stuff?" she asks with a slight pause, and then she gently raises her soft, puppy-dog brown eyebrows and lets out a soft ha, ha, har. I tug at my ball cap, feeling my Frankenstein hair. Already, it's not as stiff. Mom's special laugh tells me she is on my side, after all.

Chapter 6

Underwear Is a Good Thing

Paper ... check.

Pencil ... check.

Quiet place to think ... check.

Ideas ... no check. My worst fear has come true. I am out of ideas.

The blank piece of paper sits there haunting me. I squeeze the pencil tighter in my hand, fingers sweaty. A waffle from breakfast sits heavy in my stomach. I squirm in my seat for what seems like hours, hopelessly drawing only a few lines on the paper.

"Cripes. It's not more than a stick figure," I say out loud, even though no one is around to hear me. I let out a long, low groan as I drop my head and bonk it on top of the picnic table with a thud. I have been trying to design my Halloween costume. It's my favorite holiday, and I like to get an early start on the planning. But, today I'm having a tough time.

Slowly, I lift my head, open one eye and peek at the meek figure on the paper. Maybe I should make it funny? Or freaky? Or scary? Or, on second thought, maybe I should stop trying to make a Halloween costume and count the spokes on my bike or some other easy task.

Taking a deep breath, though, I decide to tough it out and push on.

And then it happens. Freckles zips by on her bike. "Hello, Sweetie!" she calls, her voice echoes through the tall pine trees. I thought this empty campsite was a secret spot because it is hidden by trees. Clearly I was mistaken because I can see her shiny shoes sparkle as she pedals around me. And she is wearing a dress, again. While *camping*!

Yikes! She's parking her bike and coming this way. I'm trapped. Quickly, I hide the pre-school-like drawing with my hands.

"Hey, Sweetie! What are you doing all by yourself?" Freckles asks.

As she skips toward me, her pink-ribbon-wrapped braids swing across her shoulders, and I remember when those braids gave me the idea for a candy-filled basket for Crazy Day fun. Hmm. Maybe this girl can help me after all.

"I'm making a costume," I tell her.

"How can you make a costume? We're in the middle of the woods." Freckles waves her arm across the empty lot.

"I like to do my thinking where it's quiet," I say, and without realizing it, I put the pencil in my mouth.

"Don't bite on it."

"Hey, that's what my mom tells me," I say, removing the pencil from my mouth.

"Yup. And I bet you get in trouble when she finds chewed up pencils," Freckles states.

"How did you know?"

"My mom doesn't like it when I chew on them, either," she says. "And, even though I have a sister, my mom thinks I'm the one who leaves the pencil bites."

"Your sister sounds like my brother, Brian. He's smooth. Somehow, Mom never catches him with a pencil in his mouth," I say.

"My sister is smooth, too. Get this, last night we both put our gum on the bedpost. And guess what?"

"Your sister's gum is still on the post this morning, but your gum is mysteriously - -"

"Stuck in my hair!" Freckles finishes the sentence before I can.

Freckles and I have a lot in common, it seems, and maybe we could be friends. But, I've never played with a girl. The thought of it makes the breakfast waffle in my stomach flip.

"So what are you going to make for a costume?" Freckles leans forward, wrinkles her nose, and sneers at what little of the stick figure she can see.

"Ah, well ..." I uncover part of the drawing and add a shirt. "Um ... last year for Halloween I was an astronaut and made a space helmet. And another year, a pirate with a swashbuckler's sword."

"So what's the problem now?" Freckles' sea-green eyes dart away from the drawing for a moment and zero in on me. "You'll look silly wearing that plain-looking thing."

Instantly, I feel my face heat up and redden. My stomach twists and turns making my breakfast waffle feel like I'm on a merry-go-round. I want to hide my head in shame. Why do I have to be out of ideas? Pretending to know what I'm doing, I make a few strokes at the bottom of the shirt.

"Hey, that looks like fringe," Freckles says.

"Yeah, like what a Native American Indian would wear," I say. Suddenly, my mind spins. "And look, war paint on his face, and to hold weapons, an arrow quiver, plus a headdress!" How lucky I am Freckles came along. Now I'll have the best costume for Halloween trick or treating.

"Make the headdress out of feathers," Freckles says. "I love feathers and glue and glittery beads."

Uh-oh. I'd look funny wearing feathers that twinkle. How do I get out of this crazy princess craft project? My eyes scan the campsite and look for something, anything to help me think of a way out of this mess.

"Um ... well ... I think the headdress can wait. The arrows should be first. You know, made of sticks and stones," I say.

"Oh, yeah. Stones for the arrow tips. But what will you use for the holder? I have lots of purses," she says.

I gasp. Carrying a girls' purse would be worse than beaded feathers. "How about if we use something from nature," I say, recalling Mom's weaving project.

"How'll we use nature to make a purse?" Freckles asks.

"We simply hike in the woods and look for supplies. My mom is an artist and she taught me how."

"Ooo-la-la. Your mom is an artist?" Freckles' voice sings dramatically. She must think being an artist is better than being an actress.

"Yeah, Mom will sew the Indian top and pants for me. She can work magic with a sewing machine," I say, thinking about the hum of the machine as she zips along the seams. "Every year she sews costumes from my ideas."

"You mean you don't buy them at a store?"

"Nope. We make them," I say.

"Ah, that's darling. So where should we hike for treasures and things?"

"Well, the other loop has a lot more trees," I say. We're standing in the first loop of the two- section campground.

"All right, but I'll have to tell my mom I'm going to Loop Two," she says, turning toward her bike but then stopping when she hears me give a little howl.

"Why are you laughing?"

"That's funny," I say. "My mom likes to keep track of me, too. I call her Mrs. Safety."

Freckles giggles and then nods in agreement. "Let's meet back here, without the bikes. We'll take the shortcut," she says and rides away.

I jog back to the camper.

"Hello! Hello! I'm back," I call out. No answer. It's an empty camper. I figure Mom and Brian are on the bike trails along Lake Michigan. That was their plan. But not me, I picked something different, something better – making my Halloween costume.

After leaving a note about my plan, I'm off to the meeting place. Sure enough, Freckles is waiting.

"Hey, Sweetie," she greets me.

"My name is Adam," I say.

"Okay, Sweetie." Just like that she turns to lead the way. She doesn't call me Adam, and she doesn't tell me her name. She also doesn't look back. Freckles simply marches ahead on the sandy path that leads to Loop Number Two, and I follow a few paces behind.

"Let's cut through Lot 132. It's empty, and it leads into the woods," I say.

"That sounds like a good idea." She stays in the lead and we march single file into the woods.

"Look, there's a birch tree," I say.

"Oh my, yes. It has that lovely black and white bark." We hustle over to the tree for a closer look.

"Some bark should have fallen onto the ground. Can you help me search for a piece?" I brush mounds of dead leaves aside with my foot. The dry leaves crunch and crackle as I search for the paper-thin, curly bark.

"Oh! How lucky! I see a piece." Freckles squats and snatches the bark.

"That'll make a perfect arrow quiver," I say, gazing at the round shape in her hand. But what is she doing?

Instantly, Freckles slaps the bark around her wrist and then, get this, she waves her arm in the air. "Ooo-la-la," she sings. "It looks like one of my bracelets." Now she spins in a circle. The skirt of her dress whirls like a Hoola hoop.

I scrunch up my nose. "Is this what it's like to play with a girl?" I mutter to myself and blow out a sigh. Then I try to distract her. "Next, we need to find some straight sticks to make the arrows."

"Oh, my, yes, the arrows." Freckles stops twirling and we hike deeper into the woods.

"Can you smell that?" Freckles asks as she takes in a deep breath to fill her lungs with air.

"What?"

"The oodles of pine needles. They smell delightful," she says. "But where are the trees with leaves and sticks?"

"Maybe up ahead," I say. We wander deeper into the pine forest searching for sticks.

"It's cool in all these dark shadows." Freckles huddles a little closer to me.

"And creepy," I say, inching ahead, squinting in the blackness of the dense forest. The eerie silence gives me a bad feeling in my stomach. If this place were in a storybook, there'd be witches in the woods – the kind that eat kids. The smart thing to do would be to turn around, take off fast, and not look back. But since I have a long history of rarely doing the smart thing, I take another step forward into the darkness.

Up ahead, the path curves. I can't see around the bend. My pulse quickens. Freckles is at my heels, staying so close I can feel her breath on my neck. Slowly, I creep around the last giant pine tree.

"There it is!"

"Finally, an oak tree," Freckles says and lets out a gush of air.

We jog over to the big, thick trunk. Above our heads, like an umbrella, leaves and branches fan out. And under our feet – bingo – there are lots of sticks.

"These are perfect for making arrows." I reach for a long, slender, silver-barked branch.

"Stop! Is that a snake?"

Stunned, we stare at the ground.

"Eek! A blue racer!" she cries out, frozen in place.

It's a snake, all right. And it's four times fatter than all the sticks we've been gathering. Plus it is really, really long! Longer than I am tall!

Michigan blue racers are one of the largest and fastest snakes around. They sleep at night and slither and strike in the daytime.

"Don't worry, blue racers aren't poisonous. You'll be okay," I say, mouth dry. But it doesn't feel okay to me as my heart thumps wildly in my chest.

"I know it's not deadly," Freckles says. "Besides, I bring garter snakes to show-and-tell."

"Yeah, but this snake is monster-size!" I cry.

Worse yet, its tail begins to shake like a buzzing rattle. Then its huge head arches off the ground, higher than a foot. Its piercing black eyes fix on us. Suddenly, it zaps out its long purple tongue. That does it! I dart out of there before the snake attacks. A blue racer's bite is more painful than ten thousand bee stings.

When I finally slow down, Freckles is by my side. Without the snake. Whew! I wipe my sweaty forehead with my T-shirt thinking how glad I am the snake didn't bite my arm off. There must be an angel watching over me.

"Hey, we're on a different path," Freckles says as she looks at a clump of trees with leaves instead of thick pines.

"It's okay. The campground is just through those trees." I point ahead.

"Good, it's time for me to head home." Freckles tosses me the birch bark bracelet and skips off. Just like that, she's gone without one comment about the beastly snake that almost ate us. I wonder if all girls are like Freckles.

Then I see it. Up ahead is just what I need – a massive oak tree with sticks lying everywhere. And they're easy to see in the sandy soil all around. No darkness. No leaves. No snakes. With delight, I pick up sticks until my arms are full. The bundle towers up to my face so I walk zigzag back toward the campsite.

Oomph. I bump into someone. "Who's there?" I ask.

"It's me." I recognize Red's voice. "Can I help ya with the campfire, Adam?"

Oh, boy. Red thinks I'm gathering kindling-size sticks to start a fire.

"This is more important than a silly old campfire. I'm going to use these sticks to make arrows for a costume. Here, take a couple." I squat so Red can take a few sticks from the top of the pile.

"Hey, yer gluey hair isn't stuck straight up anymore," Red notices. He should know stuck up hair, too. His frizzy, fire-engine-red hair spikes like a porcupine. "Whew, I was afraid ya might have to shave yer head," Red says.

"Luckily, it wasn't that bad," I say. Somehow, I need to change the subject away from that embarrassing moment. "Look what I'm making." I point at the drawing of the arrows.

Red's mouth drops wide open. He does this a lot.

"Close your mouth or you'll catch flies," I say.

Red snaps his jaw shut. I knew he'd get a kick out of hearing about the Halloween costume. Then, for the first time today, I look at Red. I mean really look at him. From head to toe, the little guy is covered in bright blue Superman Band-Aids.

"What's with all the Band-Aids?" I ask, hoping he didn't get hurt crashing his bike or something.

"Oh, these?" Red shows off his arms and legs that sport more than ten Band-Aids. "I like to look at my favorite superhero."

I crack up over that. Here I thought I liked action figures, but Red is a walking shrine to his favorite hero.

"So, Adam, can I help ya make the costume?" Red asks and taps the drawing.

"Oh, yeah, the Halloween costume. We need to make arrows." I shake my head to chase away the thoughts of Red's Band-Aid silliness and focus on the project at hand. "Bring me heap-big pebbles for arrow tips."

"Me Little Scout. I go," Red says. He gets into the act, too, as he pretends to mount a horse and gallop off. The small patches of bright blue Band-Aids fade into the sunset.

With Red on task, I decide to work on the quiver to hold the arrows. I dart into the camper and hunt through Mom's Treasure Drawer. It's a place where she saves the craziest stuff. Grandma calls Mom a pack rat. But because of Mom's treasure-junk, I find a prize – an empty can.

Back outside, I wrap the birch bark around the can. It looks like a genuine Indian quiver for my arrows.

Red returns with small stones. With dental floss that I snagged from the bathroom earlier, I wind and secure the stones onto the sticks and in a jiffy, we have arrows.

Now to make the last prop, the headdress.

"Hey, Little Scout," I say to Red. "Let's gather feathers from the little beach."

He nods in agreement.

I grab my baseball cap since I don't want seagull poop on my head again. My nose wrinkles as I recall the stink of that bird doo-doo.

"Don't forget the secret weapon," Red says.

"Oh, yeah." How could I forget the cheese puffs? I dash into the camper, snatch the ammo and race back outside.

"Do we have something to carry the feathers in?" Red asks.

"Right here." I grab two toy sand buckets from the beach basket stored under the camper. We hit the path that leads to Muskegon Lake shoreline, the smaller lake that flows into big Lake Michigan.

"Remember, we can't go into the water. Just stay on the beach," I say.

"I know, I know. I'm too little to swim without a grown-up," Red says.

For the most part, Muskegon Lake is shallow for a long distance and the waves tend to be low-key, unlike the big, rough, dangerous ones over on the Big Lake. The best part about the little lake and its calm shoreline is that it's filled with hidden keepsakes. Shells, fossils, and crayfish skeletons all collect there. Today, however, we are on a hunt for feathers.

Following the sandy path that cuts through Loop Two, we arrive at the little beach.

"Ready to launch the secret weapon?" Red asks.

"Fire away." I toss a pocketful of cheese puffs into the air. The seagulls flock for the orange treats.

"Now?" Red asks.

"Not quite yet. Wait a minute longer."

"Now?"

"Okay, now." Red and I give out a holler, wave our hands high in the air, and run toward the birds. The seagulls squawk and fly away. Holy cow. It's a bonanza of feathers.

"Adam, look at this," Red says.

"What a catch! That's not from a seagull." The feather is more than a foot long. It must be from a trumpeter swan, which can be bigger than a Thanksgiving turkey.

Red pokes the feather in his hair. "Adam, me no more Little Scout, me Big White Feather," he says and struts, doing a high-stepping march.

We bring the buckets of feathers back to the campsite. Now the tricky part. How to make a headdress of a hundred feathers stay on my head?

I grab the drawing pad and sit at the picnic table. By flicking my fingers, the pencil raps on the blank paper. I chew the pencil, but remember not to leave any teeth marks. What can I use to keep the headdress on my head? I drum the eraser on the paper. With each tap, the eraser hits harder. Jeepers. My mind is empty.

"I'm bored," Red says. The feather in his hair has blown away. The excitement of being Big White Feather has faded. He slowly heads home, shuffling his feet in the sand.

As I sit at the picnic table, I slip off my blue and orange ball cap. It's my newest one – Detroit Tigers with a fancy letter D front and center. I have a soft spot for this hat because I got to pick it out myself earlier this summer when we took a trip to Comerica Park to watch the Tigers play.

Flipping the cap over, I examine the inside and notice a band running around the rim. That's what I need: a headband. But I don't have one. I could tightly tie a scarf around my head, but that would just give me a headache on Halloween night. Yet if the band is too loose, it will drop and fall into my eyes. I need to see to grab all that candy.

The blank sheet of paper glares at me. I twirl the pencil between my fingers, and run the eraser through my hair. Hmm. What would a famous inventor do? Ben Franklin was smart about methods. I smile to myself. Ben Franklin sounds like my brother, Brian. Well, let's see, first they would think and ponder. But I've already done that. This isn't going to be easy.

I decide to list the important parts:
Something stretchy.
Not too tight.

Not too loose.

Something just right.

Then it comes to me. I run into the camper for the bucket of old clothes we use as rags for washing the van. Mom loves to save cotton fabric for rags. There's that word again – save. If I find what I need, that will be twice today Pack-Rat Mom has come to the rescue.

I snag the rag bucket out from under the kitchen sink. The hunt is on. First, there is an old T-shirt. I toss it out. Next, an old flannel pajama top. Not quite right. I fling it aside. Digging deeper, with almost my whole head in the bucket, I find exactly what I'm looking for.

From the kitchen drawer, I grab scissors. Snip. Trim. Snip. Within minutes, I have a stretchy band, cut from the waist of an old pair of ... underwear. My throat feels tight, it's hard to swallow. What if Brian discovers my secret? This would be more embarrassing than mustache wax in my hair or seagull poop on my head. My face gets so hot my ears burn. I can imagine Brian chanting mean things: "I see London, I see France, on Adam's head are underpants!" I feel the thump, thump of my heart wildly pound in my chest. What if I get caught? I examine the elastic band once more.

The waistband is from a pair of navy blue underwear. And, the label is removed. It's worth the risk, I decide, and slip the band onto my head.

Not too loose.

Not too tight.

And not white!

I grab glue from the craft drawer and paste on seagull feathers. When the last feather is stuck on, I have more than a hundred feathers in place.

Slipping the headdress on, I put my shoulders back and stand straight as an arrow. The feathers stretch up to the stars. Instantly, I have grown two feet taller, without even being on tiptoes.

"Wow! What a cool headdress! Those feathers are fantastic!" Brian says. I hadn't heard him come into the camper. He reaches up and gently pats my feathers like they are jewels on a king's crown.

I agree and say, "It's just right."

Chapter 7

Cooking for a Caveman

Elmo.

A firefighter, a sheriff, G.I. Joe.

A bad guy, all in black.

An astronaut, a mummy.

And, my favorite, Batman.

I am reciting all the past Halloween costumes I've made to see if it helps me come up with an idea for Brian. I have already made the coolest props for my own costume, to be a Native American Indian. There is an over-the-shoulder birch-bark quiver, complete with stone-tipped arrows. And a headdress with so many feathers they hang down my back, almost to the floor. But, better yet is the clever trick I used for the headband.

"How did you make the headdress stay on your head?" Brian asked.

"Uh, I found some stretchy fabric," I said, determined never to tell what the mystery fabric is for the headband. It feels good to be one step ahead of my brother.

To make Brian happy, though, I told him I'd help him whip up a great Halloween costume of his own. So here I am, lying on my back under an oak tree at our campsite, working on ideas. I think about Brian's costumes in past Halloweens. He has been a clown, Cookie Monster and a police officer. Once, he was a Master of Disguise. This one involved having more than twenty different hats, like the Mad Hatter. He's also been a pirate and a wizard. I have to admit, Brian does great costumes, too.

"Fetch!" I hear Red yell to his playful dog, Slick. I look over to Red's campsite and see Slick chasing the stick that Red just tossed. He snatches it off the ground and prances back with his head high, teeth clenching his prize. But Slick doesn't fetch quite right. Instead, he struts right past Red and trots to a cozy spot in the shade with his stick.

"Here Slick. Come here, boy!" Red calls and claps his hands.

"I guess Slick doesn't want to play fetch," I say to Red, from my own comfy spot under the shade tree. Our campsites are side-by-side.

"I guess not. Maybe it's too hot," Red says. "But, hey, Adam, what are ya doing?"

"Trying to help Brian."

"Golly. How ya doing that by lying there?" Red scratches his head in puzzlement.

"By thinking up a Halloween costume for him to wear this year," I say.

"Oh boy! One with feathers and stones and things?" Red's voice squeals with excitement.

"Kind of. But this costume will be different from mine."

"So what'll Brian be?" Red asks, leaning in close like he doesn't want to miss hearing the answer.

"Well, I'm not sure."

Red steps back. "Maybe ya need yer drawing pad like the last time."

"Nah, today I'll just think," I say, deciding it feels good to relax and do nothing under the shade of the old oak.

"Well, good luck with that, Adam," Brian says with a bite to his words.

Where did he come from? Instantly, I sit up. I turn my head toward the sound of his voice. Oh no. I see my brother get off his bike and head toward us.

"You've been thinking about my costume for two days," Brian snarls. His cougar-like green eyes are sharp, sucking me in, and chewing me up like catnip.

"What's the hurry? It's a three-week vacation," I say, trying to buy some time.

"With one week gone already!" he snaps back while scuffing off into the camper to end the conversation.

"He just wishes he had a headdress like mine," I say to Red. It's unusual for Brian to lose his cool. Generally, he's rock steady. Of course, it is an awesome headdress, I admit to myself rather proudly.

"So what's Brian gonna be?" Red asks again.

I gaze at the clouds above my head and squint thoughtfully. Maybe I'll see a face, or a figure, or a shape of some kind to inspire my imagination. But there's nothing there. I let out a slow groan of frustration.

"Guess I'll get that drawing pad after all." I push myself up off the ground.

"I think a book with a lot of pictures might help, too," Red says.

Jeepers. No one has faith in me. But, I'll show them. Adam Moynihan will figure this out. I can make up a new costume. I just need more time is all.

As I head to the camper, I hear Slick gnawing away. I take a few steps closer to get a better look at Slick. "Hey Red. That's not the stick you threw Slick."

"Nah, it's a bone," Red says.

"Now that's a slick trick, to run for a stick and come back with a bone," I say.

"A strange looking bone, too," Red says. We poke our noses down low to check out what Slick is drooling over.

"It looks like the kind in a science book, a leg bone – skinny in the middle and fat at each end." I ease the thing away from Slick and see that the bone almost fits in the palm of my hand.

"Except, this bone would be an itty-bitty critter's leg, not one from a dinosaur," Red says.

"Yeah, but it's probably old because it's yellow and crusty. Like it's prehistoric." That's it! I have the answer to Brian's Halloween costume! I fly into the camper.

"Brian, you can be a caveman! The costume is easy. Simply use a burlap sack with a rope tied at the waist," I explain.

"What about props?" he asks. "You've got that super-cool headdress."

"Yeah, sure. Props," I say. How could I forget about props? I grumble to myself.

On my way out the camper door, I pass my Indian headdress and stroke its soft, fluffy seagull feathers. There are more than a hundred of them. And the secret stretchy headband holds them all in place. Chief Sitting Bull would be proud to wear this. No wonder Brian wants his own props.

Let me see, cavemen hunt and fight and capture wild animals. I try to think of an idea, any idea, but my mind is blank. Empty. Zip. Only a medicine man with healing powers could get my brain working. Back outside, I pace around the fire pit.

"Now what are ya doing, Adam?" Red asks. Sometimes this little fellow stays so quiet I forget he's still here.

"I'm thinking."

"By just walking in circles?"

"It'll help me dream up a prop for Brian's caveman outfit," I say.

"Well heck, I can sprinkle sugar on yer head," Red says.

"And why do I want sugar on my head?"

"My granny says sugar is pixie dust and it'll make all yer dreams come true." This sounds like something a five-year-old would believe. Right now, though, with no ideas in my head, I wish sugar really was pixie dust. Only magic will get me out of this mess.

Crunch, crunch. I turn toward the sound and see that Slick is back to gnawing on his bone.

"Hey, Red, we don't need any sugar or pixie dust to dream up a prop," I say. "We can use Slick's bones and string them into a necklace. The bones will be Brian's caveman hunting trophies."

"Yeah, bones that Brian pretends to get from fighting wild animals." Red does a one-two punch into the air. Then he stops. "But, um, Adam."

"What?"

"Slick only has one bone," Red says.

Sadly, one bone is not enough for a caveman to brag and boast. Just then, I see Brian coming out of the camper and walking toward us. Uh-oh. This day is getting worse by the minute.

"So what'll we make for my caveman prop?" Brian asks.

"A necklace of bones ... caveman's trophies," I say.

"But where do we get the bones?" he asks.

"Uh, from Slick." It's a stretch but I don't want to admit defeat. Now I really wish I had that magic pixie dust to work hocus-pocus and turn the one bone into a pile of bones.

"Of course, a dog's sense of smell is actually a thousand times better than ours. Slick will find us more bones," Brian says.

Lacking a better plan, I play along.

"Here Slick, fetch." I toss a stick and hope he'll bring back a bone like he did earlier with Red. He trots off and brings back the same stick. I pat his soft and furry head. "Nice try," I say. "But not quite what I need." Slick cocks his shaggy head at me, yips, and spins in a circle.

"Let me try," Brian says. "Fetch!" Slick brings back the same stick.

"What's your next bright idea, Adam?" my brother asks as his jaw muscle tightens.

"Hey, you're the one who said dogs had such a great sense of smell," I say and take a step toward him. Now we're face to face and our green eyes lock. We're ready to growl at each other, but it's Slick who lets out a bark that sidetracks us.

Brian and I glance at Slick, and then back at each other. At the same time, we say together, "Throw the bone, not the stick!"

I step closer to Slick and kneel down next to him. Tail wagging hard, Slick licks my face with his tongue. It tickles and makes me giggle. I can't help myself, he's so lovable, and I wrap my arms around him and give him a big squeeze. Then I grab Slick's bone, toss it, and tell him, "Fetch." He trots off ... and brings back a stick! Ugh.

Determined not to give up, I jog after the bone, snatch it, and march up to Slick. "Yum, yum, good bone, good dog." I scratch behind his ears and put the bone under his nose. "Smell this, go get more. Fetch." I give the bone a heave.

But the same act, another stick.

Brian shakes his head in disgust. "Call me when you have a better idea." He stomps off to his bike and pedals away.

My heart sinks. I have to admit defeat. This is worse than the awful Magic Eight Ball message: *outlook not good*.

Maybe a cold drink will help. I offer Red a juice box but he just shakes his head and says, "There's not much happening around here. I'll just head home."

Red shuffles next door and I drag myself into the camper. Stepping inside I kick a forgotten marble across the floor that must have dropped out of the pouch earlier today. The marble shoots down the narrow aisle, hits the corner, and bounces back towards me. I pick up the marble and roll the smooth shiny glass ball between my fingers.

The marble pouch is tucked away in my special treasure drawer, which I yank open. Instantly I spot the conch shell Grandma gave me after solving a riddle. I put the shell to my ear and listen to the ocean roar. The echo calms like a lullaby. For the moment my problem with Brian's costume fades away. Then I look out the camper window and see him zoom by on his bike. I slip the shell in my pocket, head back outside, and plunk down on the picnic table. How do I find more bones?

My head hangs low as I try to figure out what to do next. Then, without warning, I hear a snort and look up to see Hulk stomping up. This is the big guy who blasted Red with a water balloon at our carnival game. Hulk plays by his own rules, and the rest of us don't know them, so whenever he's around I stay cautious.

"Hey, what goes?" Hulk is the master of the three-word sentence.

"Uh ..." I look up – way up – at him. Hulk is twice as tall as I am. "Just working on a Halloween costume idea."

"What's it gonna to be?" he asks, bending over so low that his brown hair scratches my nose. It's like staring at the fur of a bear. A giant brown grizzly bear.

"Ah ..." My mouth is dry and my tongue feels too big to talk through. I lick my numb lips and somehow manage to say, "A caveman. Who wears bones as trophies."

"Huh? You're gonna wear chicken bones?" He stands up and lets out a laugh so deep it comes from the bottom of his gut. The hearty laugh bellows across the campground.

I stare at Hulk with wonder, because this giant just came up with the answer!

"Gotta go," I say, stepping forward instead of back and accidentally crashing right into the big guy. The force sends me to the ground, landing on my butt. I scurry back onto my feet, nod a thank you, and dash into the camper. I'm not sure if I'm happier I have my Halloween problem solved or if I'm happier to be away from the grizzly bear whose stare gives me goose bumps.

Inside the camper, Mom is at the kitchen sink snapping beans for dinner. I shove my hands in my pockets and rock on my heels. Could I be so lucky that Mom bought chicken at the grocery store? "Hey, Mom. Do we have any chicken legs we could cook for dinner?" Inside my pockets, I wiggle my sweaty fingers nervously, waiting for an answer. That's when I feel the conch shell and give it a rub for good luck.

Mom nods, "Yes, in fact, I am planning to have a chicken cookout tonight."

I can't believe my luck. I rub the shell again. "How many do we have?"

"Expecting company?" she asks.

"No, but I've got this great idea."

Mom's electric blue eyes shoot my way, and they're sparking with interest. She knows about my great ideas. "A great idea – like when you tried to catch squirrels by casting the fishing pole off the balcony at Grandma's?" she asks.

"I only snagged her rosebush once," I reply.

"Is that why rose petals were flying in every direction?" The electric current in Mom's eyes is at full power. Probably more than a hundred watts.

Mom doesn't always like my great ideas, but I keep trying. In my pocket, I rub the conch shell to power a little of Mom's energy into good luck. "Brian wants to be a caveman for Halloween, so he needs a warrior's necklace."

"That's nice." Her blue eyes cool to a lower voltage.

"All we need are left-over bones."

"I don't see why not."

Mom is an artist and likes it when Brian and I recycle. She calls it thinking outside the box, so I keep going. "And, we'll need rawhide to string the bones into the necklace."

"Rawhide?"

"Yeah, you know, like the strong shoelaces in hiking boots," I say.

"And whose hiking boots have rawhide laces?" she asks. We both know Mom's boots are the ones with these laces.

"We could buy you new laces the next time we go to town," I suggest.

"I see." Mom takes a step toward me. She is so close her brown, shoulder-length hair swishes above my head. Instantly I get a whiff of her special Mom shampoo – peaches and cream. She snatches me in her arms, snuggles me and says, "Just remember to write 'laces' on the shopping list. We don't want to forget to buy them."

"You bet." I go and grab her boots while thinking that I should carry the lucky conch shell everywhere I go.

After dinner, Brian and I offer to clean up the dinner dishes while Mom puts her feet up outside.

In the camper, using kitchen tongs, Brian plucks at a half-eaten piece of chicken. "This is gross!" He holds up a chicken leg. Meat still clings to the bone. "How can I wear this around my neck?" I'll have cats chasing me."

Jeepers. Another problem. Then I remember when Grandma Barb canned tomatoes. She boiled the tomatoes so the skin fell off. If boiling works for tomatoes, it must work for chicken bones. "You won't wear them like this," I say. "We'll cook them."

"But the chicken is already cooked," Brian says, a bit puzzled.

"No, no, I mean we'll boil the bones so all the meat falls off."

Brian shakes his head. "What are you talking about?"

"Just watch, it's a great idea." I search wildly through the cupboard for a big pot. I pull out the huge kettle we use to boil sweet corn, lug it to the sink, and fill it with water. I grunt, trying to move the brimming pot. "Help me lift this."

Brian and I each grab a handle. I grit my teeth and lift with all my might. We heave the pot out of the sink and move it toward the stove. "Almost there," I say.

Then, an inch from the burner, the bottom of the pot hits the edge of the stove. Sploosh. Instantly, I'm drenched. And, if that's not enough – Mom walks in. No one moves. No one blinks. Just me standing there, drip, drip, drip, with a water puddle at my feet.

Brian is only inches away from me yet he's bone dry.

"If you so much as crack a smile, it's all over," I say to my brother.

The corner of Brian's mouth twitches a little, telling me he is smiling on the inside. I want to shove an oven mitt in his mouth.

Mom looks at me and says, "I can't believe it always happens to you, Adam. Are you okay?"

"Yeah, I'm okay, but I have the worst luck. First, Slick doesn't fetch any bones. Then, we get bones only a cat would love."

Mom giggles and Brian bursts out laughing. I join in as I realize how silly the day has been.

Looking down at my T-shirt and shorts, I press a towel against them. There is no reason to change clothes, because the warm evening air will dry them soon enough. Brian and I mop up the water on the floor.

We fill the pot once again, and this time Mom helps us move it to the stove. Brian turns the knob and a gas flame whooshes on. Plop, plunk, plop goes the water as I drop in the bones. Our caveman plan is back on schedule. I grab a big wooden spoon, dip it into the pot, and stir the bones so they're swirling around.

"They'll cook faster with the lid on the pot," Brian says, batting at my spoon with the lid in his hand. "Besides, it'll take a while to heat so much water."

"That's fine," I say, ready to relax.

"Now, what about my caveman tool?" Brian asks.

I can't believe my brother wants more. Why aren't a burlap-sack costume and a warrior necklace enough? Maybe I should surrender and tell him about the mystery headband fabric on my headdress and get myself out of this mess of having to help him invent props.

I hesitate and shove my hand in my pocket. The lucky conch shell. I give it a rub and then ask, "Uh ... what kind of tool?"

"A club, of course!"

I let out a happy sigh and give the conch shell a gentle pat of thanks. "A club is a great idea."

Thank goodness my brother is taking charge again. Until now, I never knew how much I liked that.

"Sure, to make the club we can use rawhide lace to wrap a rock around a stick," he says.

"Okay, but there aren't many rocks around with all this sand," I say.

Brian is quick with an answer. "We can use one of your arrow rocks, Adam."

At the idea of sharing, I twist my face into an ugly frown. Mom catches the look and says to me, "If I have to share my rawhide laces you can share a rock or two."

I suppose it'll be easier to share arrow rocks than to take a heap of razzing and teasing from Brian if he finds out about the mystery headband fabric.

Brian unlaces Mom's hiking boots while I unwrap one of the arrows. Skillfully, Brian crisscrosses the rawhide and secures the rock to the stick. "Grrrrh," he grunts like a caveman as he whips the club through the air.

Around the campground, Brian creeps and crawls while he jabs his caveman club at imaginary wild animals. I sit quietly at the picnic table, glad the thinking-up part of Halloween is finished.

"Time to check the bones," Mom says, and we hustle into the camper kitchen. "Are you ready to peek in the pot?" Mom lifts the lid.

"Wow!" I say. The simmering water has cleaned the bones smoother than if Slick chewed them for a week.

"I'll pour out the hot water," Mom says. I guess she's had enough spills for one day.

After they cool and dry, Brian gathers the bones and takes Mom's other rawhide lace to tie a square knot around each bone. Lastly, he knots the two ends to form the necklace.

"Look at me, look at me." Brian slips the necklace over his head. Twelve bones dangle on his chest like wild game trophies. Grabbing his club, he raises it high in the air. The swift movement causes his caveman's necklace to rattle.

I slip on my headdress and join him, strutting in a circle to parade my headdress of more than a hundred feathers. I'm never telling Brian I have underwear on my head. And I'm never giving up my lucky conch shell.

Chapter 8

Silence Says It All

Pedaling my five-speed mountain bike at lightning speed, I aim at the target. The wide front tire rams straight into the blacktop pothole. Bull's eye! I sail through the air, jerk the handlebars, spin a "180" half circle, and land in the sand, kicking up dust.

Who ever thought I could find the same thrill I get snowboard jumping during the summer? In the winter, at Dad's place in Spring Lake, we go out to the local ski bowl called Mulligan's Hollow. The runs, which are short and kind of puny, are carved out of a small sand dune, and a jerky rope tow is what chugs us to the top of the hill. Blasting down the short run takes only seconds.

"The Bowl" at Mulligan's Hollow really isn't that much of a thrill. Luckily, though, there is a secret weapon at The Bowl: Groomer Man. He works his magic with Piston

Bully, the snow-grooming machine he uses to push piles of snow into a giant mound. Then we have some fun sailing over the heaps of snow doing spins and flips and tricks.

Right now, though, without snow, without a ski hill, without a snowboard, I bust out jumps and tricks by flying through the air on a dirt bike.

"How many times are you going to practice that jump?" Brian asks as he lies on his back under a shade tree.

"All day!"

I pedal around for another jump.

Earlier this morning, I discovered a huge pothole in the blacktop at Campsite No. 37. Ordinarily the pad is used to park a camper, but this lot is empty. So when I pedal at high speed and roll in and out of the pothole, I catch air on my bike.

"Do you think I could jump higher if I wedge a campfire log in front of the pothole?" I ask Brian, wanting to jump higher.

"Yeah, you'd probably get more lift with a log or two." He rolls over onto his stomach like he's going to take a nap.

For some reason, my brother doesn't get excited about jumps and tricks. During the winter while I'm snowboarding, Brian skis. Like a robot, he plants, leans, and turns down the hill. Sometimes he races through gates. Brian says the thrill for him is to beat the time clock. But it is always the same plant-lean-turn down the hill. Boring. How can he not love snowboarding? It has more variety than pizza has toppings.

Dust flies behind me as I pedal out of the sand toward another jump just as I hear Mom calling for us. Darn. I've barely done thirty tricks. I wonder what she wants.

"Perfect timing," Brian says, "Mom needs us before you get thrown like a bronco buster."

I grumble to myself as I pedal back to camp. My action-packed adventure will have to be put on hold. Once off the bike, I feel a trail of sweat drip down my back.

Stepping into the camper, Mom looks up from cleaning a counter. Her eyes travel over every inch of me and stop on my face. There is a tiny spark in her eyes. "Adam, why are you so hot and sweaty and dirty?" she asks.

"You know I always get sweaty riding my bike when it's this sticky outside." I decide to play it safe and skip the part about flying through the air like a rocket.

"Well, today certainly is humid," she remarks, and the spark in her eyes fades.

Whew. I'm glad I could snuff out that spark before it blazed. Mom, Mrs. Safety, probably would get nervous about tricks on a bike. She calls snowboarding an extreme sport, but I think for Mom, worrying is an extreme sport.

"Go wash up so we can leave for Farmer Frank's," Mom says. "The sweet corn is ready."

Ah, sweet corn. I should have guessed this is why Mom called us. Each summer, in August, one of Mom's favorite foods is an ear of corn, picked fresh and immediately shucked, boiled, and eaten.

After a quick splash of cold water on my face and change of T-shirt, I get into the van with Mom and Brian.

"How long do you think we'll be gone?" I ask Mom.

"Not too long. Just this one stop," she says.

Hooray! I can't wait to get back to camp to be an air dog again. Maybe do a full 360 spin. We roll along Memorial Drive. Riding co-pilot, I squint into the summer sun. The warm rays fuel my dirt bike daydreams. Lost in thoughts of spins and tricks, I don't pay attention to Brian and Mom chatting about some dark clouds off in the distance.

Shortly we turn onto a rural road, and the bumpy ride jerks me out of my fantasy. Gravel crunches under the tires and a cloud of dust whirls behind us as the van rattles down the long road. Farmer Frank's is off the beaten path.

Miles of tall, green corn sway in the rustling wind. I put down the window, and a wave of summer heat tickles my face. The air smells like freshly baked cornbread.

Soon the farm is in sight, and we park between the barn and farmhouse. When I open the passenger door and hop out, a strange thing happens. An unexpected wind slams the van door shut behind me and whips against my face, making my eyes water. I look up to see huge dark clouds, now directly overhead.

Mom fights the wind as she struggles toward me using the side of the van to hold steady as she walks. Brian is latched onto her, creeping behind. Mom grabs hold of my hand and we all huddle close together in the powerful wind.

"Skedaddle over here!" calls Farmer Frank as he hangs onto his straw hat for dear life. The hat is a big part of Frank's farm uniform, along with the bib overalls and a weathered face that's wrinkled and puckered like a sun-dried raisin. "Get a move on!" Farmer Frank yells in his scratchy voice. He struggles to hold open a wooden door to a small barn.

Out in the field, the wicked wind easily whips the sturdy corn plants every which way. Dust from the road blows up into our faces, so we keep our heads down to fight the gritty wind and hustle inside the barn with its weathered paint and sagging roof.

"We're fixin' for a storm, with this hot, humid weather," Farmer Frank shouts over the roar of the wind outside. "I saw the radar on the Internet. It's flashing a tornado watch."

A tornado? Time stands still for several heartbeats as I picture getting sucked up in this little barn by a black funnel cloud like Dorothy in "The Wizard of Oz."

"Don't go getting all riled up. I reckon we'll be safe in the root cellar." Farmer Frank's shouting pulls me out of my trance just as he waves us over to shelter.

The clouds are twice as dark now. In fact, the entire sky is black, but, whew, no funnel cloud. Mom pushes us forward as another gust of wind whips by. Farmer Frank pushes hard against the rough wooden barn door to keep it from swinging in the wild wind. The rusty door hinges groan and then one of them snaps free, sending metal parts sailing. The broken hinge flaps and rattles as the door rocks in the wicked wind, but Farmer Frank holds tight.

"Hurry up, folks," he hollers, and then grabs my arm to boost me up into the barn.

The barn, I learn is a corn crib. It's dark inside except for slits of daylight from the narrow rays of weak light from the stormy sky that seep in between the weathered boards that hang sideways, like the wood is lying down and sleeping. Except for a few dried up corn husks crunching under our feet, the barn is empty.

Farmer Frank is the last one inside. He tugs at the door, but the powerful wind fights back. It finally slams shut but hangs crooked from the broken hinge. Quickly, Farmer Frank slides a latch pin in place and the door holds tight.

"Come this way!" Frank shouts. "There's a shed attached to this here barn, and there's a root cellar. We'll be safe, I reckon!"

I don't know what a root cellar is, but there is no time to ask questions as the fierce wind whistles through the wooden slats. It growls at us like a mean wolf, ready to blow this corn crib in. I wish we were in the three little pigs' house of bricks instead of this one built of sticks.

Frank hurries us to the back of the corn-crib barn. He twists a rusty doorknob and gives it a mighty tug that snaps the door open. Without wasting a second, Frank puts his hand on my back and hustles me into a small, wooden cubbyhole of a space.

This must be the shed, and it's not much bigger than a doghouse for a big mutt. Above my head is a small window covered in grime, and the threatening storm hisses through a crack in the glass, sending a chill down my spine.

"The root cellar is down those steps!" Frank barks. He pokes me to move forward.

Peering down the steps in the shed, it is completely dark. I can't see beyond the first three steps. Cool air scrapes against my face, and I feel the dampness of the cellar rising up the stairs. What a smell! It stinks like a soggy-wet baseball mitt forgotten in the trunk of a car. If there wasn't a chance of a tornado outside, I'd turn and flee this dark place – fast.

"Hit the light switch," Farmer Frank says from behind us.

When I flip the switch, a dim light barely glows from the bottom of the dungeon-like stairwell. The wooden steps of the cellar creak under my feet. There is no handrail, so I press my palm against the rough wall, feeling dirt crumble between my fingers when I touch the soft spaces between the bricks.

The root cellar is lit by a single electric bulb hanging from a wire. It casts dark shadows that creep across the dirt floor. I am the first one to enter, and I'm glad the others are right behind me in this spooky space.

Suddenly, kaboom! Lightning strikes very close outside. I jump and stumble over several baskets of potatoes, carrots, and beets stacked in a corner.

"Watch out for the root vegetables," Brian says. He stands so close behind me I feel his warm breath on my neck.

"The what?" I ask focusing on what scary critter might be living down here rather than the vegetables I tripped over.

"We store crops in this here cellar where it's cool year round," Farmer Frank says.

Outside, another crack of lightning explodes nearby and shoots a flash of bright light. My legs wobble under me, so I sink to the cold, damp dirt floor. Brian sits down next to me. Above us, thunder roars and rumbles as quarter-size pellets of rain slam against the shed and the wind rattles the window. I inch a bit closer to my brother.

"How long do you think we'll need to stay down here?" I choke out the words like I have one of Frank's potatoes stuck in my throat.

"I figure the storm will pass by half-past the hour," Farmer Frank says.

Gosh, that sounds like a long time from now, I think.

"Half-past the hour is about forty minutes," Mom says, checking her watch.

Jeepers. This trip is not the short joyride I thought it would be. Visions of dirt bike jumping any time soon begin to fade.

When I pull my knees up to my chest to hug, one hand brushes a cargo pocket and I feel a bump there. What's that? I shove my hand in and feel the conch shell that Grandma Barb gave me. After figuring out Brian's Halloween costume, I decided the shell was a lucky charm and have started carrying it with me. I close my eyes; give it a rub, and wait. Among the hiss of the wind and the beating peck-peck of rain pellets against the glass window, I hear my brother's calm and steady voice.

"Summer storms are usually quick to blow over," Brian says. "It's simply the hot sun mixing with Lake Michigan cool water temperatures, making cumulonimbus clouds. Once the clouds burst, the storm blows over."

Brian's wise words stop the choke-hold on my throat. He doesn't realize it, but his certainty really helps relax me.

"Besides," Mom says, "a basement is the safest place to be in a tornado."

Yikes! She had to use the T-word! What if the storm blows down the shabby shed and we're trapped down here? My heart fires faster than a jackhammer.

145

Brian sees me squirm. "Wait a minute, Mom" he says. "It's a tornado watch, which means to just be on the lookout for a possible tornado."

Whew. I wipe my sweaty forehead on my shirtsleeve. So much for my thirst for dare-devil stuff. Right now I prefer Brian's simple and robotic skiing technique: "plant, lean, turn."

Brian winks at me, but doesn't say a word. Sometimes you can say a lot without saying anything at all. It is the silent language between brothers.

Time drags on. At least another ten minutes. I've sat so long, my butt is numb. I give my lucky conch shell another rub.

"Listen. The rain stopped," Brian says. I look up at the shed window at the top of the stairs. A ray of sunlight presses through the grime.

"Hear tell, I think it's over," Farmer Frank says. "Let's go check out the corn."

I am the first one to fly up the steps to escape the dark and smelly safety room.

What a change! The heavy, stormy clouds are gone, the sun is shining and the birds are singing. Only a gentle breeze brushes my face. This is the Michigan I love. And I love my lucky conch shell.

Taking in a deep breath, the crisp fresh air after the storm fills my lungs, and it feels great to be outdoors. The tall stands of sweet corn are soaking wet but still perfect to pick. No bad storm damage today. One twist and each ear of corn breaks off the stalk, so before long, we have the bushel of corn we came here to pick.

It's time to say good-bye to our hero, Farmer Frank. I clamp my arms around his waist and give him a dance-like hug, which spins him in a circle. Farmer Frank lets out a sort of rough chuckle that sounds like a croaking frog.

We take the short drive back to camp, but before I can whiz off on my bike and tackle a jump, Mom has a few chores in store for us. I have to sweep sand off the outdoor carpet we use around the picnic table.

"Hey, Adam, what are ya doing'?" It's Red, my camping sidekick.

"Just finishing a job for Mom."

"Can ya help me catch a daddy long-leg with that?"

"With this broom?" I ask, wondering why we'll need a broom to catch a spider.

"Yeah, the spider is up high."

"So why not let him be?"

"Golly, don't ya know I like to collect spiders," Red says.

I didn't know, but I'm not surprised because Red and I match a lot. We both eat frozen waffles cookie-style and often hum the same tune.

"So will ya help me catch the spider?" Red asks again.

"Okay, sure thing," I say and smile. I swing the broom handle over my shoulder and march like a soldier to Red's campsite.

"Up there," he says, pointing to a high corner where the camper and awning meet.

Way above my head, in a deep dark corner, is the largest daddy long-leg I have ever seen. His round, brown body is the size of a grape, and his legs spread out as wide as my open hand. He is the grand-daddy of daddy long-legs. No wonder Red wants to collect this big, fuzzy, eight-legger.

"That's mighty high up," I say, thinking we could use a ladder. But the only ladder I know about is the extra heavy wooden one we built. But we made the ladder into a raft and then dragged it to Red's cousin, Caleb's, on the other side of the campground, using it for a jail. So, I figure, Red is right, the broom is the best tool around.

I toss the broom into the air, toward the spider, but it sails too low and crashes to the ground.

"Now what?" Red asks.

"Well, we could find another spider." I don't want to give up the king of all daddy long-legs, but this spider is out of reach even with the broom.

"Awe, gee, Adam, can't we catch it?" Red says, shoulders sagging.

Oh boy. Looking at his puffed out lower lip and hanging head, my heart turns to pudding.

"Climb up on my shoulders," I say. Red hustles up and then grabs the broom, ready to swing at the giant spider.

"Yee-haw." Red's legs wiggle and wobble on my shoulders like he is riding a horse.

"Hold still or I'll lose my balance!"

Red grabs hold of my head to steady himself, but then his hands cover my eyes. Blindly, I sway from side to side.

"Giddyup." Red whips the broom around with his other hand in a motion like a cowhand spinning a lasso.

"Settle down! You're supposed to be hunting a spider, not rustling cattle." I try to control his cowboy kicks.

"Oh, I forgot," Red says.

"So, can you reach the spider?" I ask because I can't see with Red's hand still in my way.

"Ummp! I can almost reach it. Adam, can ya go up on yer tiptoes?"

"I'll try."

"That's great! Now, if I push the handle. Uh-oh."

"What?"

"Well. It's not good." Oh no. My breath catches. Then Red shifts too quickly. I lose my balance, and we tumble to the ground.

Flat on my back, with full vision again, I can plainly see what is "not good." The broom is stuck inside a small opening in the corner of the awning. Somehow, Red managed to shove it far out of reach. A chilly path of goose bumps runs up my arms. How am I going to explain this one to Mom?

Just then, the unthinkable happens. The giant eight-legger crawls on top of the broom bristles and slowly makes its way down the handle. When it reaches the tip, it begins to spin a web. Suddenly, the stuck-broom problem no longer matters.

"Quick, get the bug keeper ready," I say and scamper to my feet.

"What bug keeper?" Red asks.

Cripes. How does Red plan on catching a spider without a bug keeper? "Hurry, go next door. My mom saves all kinds of glass jars. They're in the recycling bin."

Red darts off and, in seconds, is back with a jar. He unscrews the lid, all the while muttering to the spider, "Come on, big fellow. I promise to feed ya a real tasty fly."

Red's charm is magical. As he holds the jar up to the web, the spider slides down its web and drops right in.

"I knew he'd like me." Red cradles the jar smiling at his new pet.

"Now, what about the broom?" I ask.

"Do ya think yer Mom will miss it?"

I nod as a cold dread crawls through my stomach. Getting the broom stuck is worse than forgetting to do my camping chores.

"Do ya have a rope? Maybe I can lasso it," Red suggests.

Shucks, after seeing Red use a broom like a lasso, I know he can't swing a rope. Right now, the only use for a rope would be for hog-tying. That's what Mom will do to me when she finds out about the broom. First hog-tied then grounded. And being grounded while camping is the worst. I have to figure out something and quick.

"Say, what's up with the broom?" A gruff, deep voice startles me from behind.

Yikes! I almost jump out of my shoes. I know that growl. Hulk stands behind me waiting for his answer.

Red skids away to hide under the picnic table which leaves me standing there all alone. Cautiously, I baby-step toward the big guy and he stomps toward me.

"Why's that broom stuck up there?" His heavy breath blows down on my face. I'd rather be skydiving without a parachute than be standing here. I swallow hard and try to answer Hulk, but my tongue sticks to the roof of my mouth and no words come out. I squeeze my eyes shut.

Maybe he'll disappear as fast as he showed up. Then I open my eyes ... but he's still there, planted in place like a lineman in football.

Finally, I find my voice and say in a squeak as high as Minnie Mouse, "Oh, the broom. Well, it's a long story."

"So the broom story's too long to tell?" Hulk sputters into my face.

Then he turns away from me, leans forward, and bends at the waist. Even folded over, he is twice as tall as me. His dark eyes glare and he points at Red, who is still under the picnic table. "Hey, little red-haired kid, come here," Hulk roars. "It's up to you to get that broom unstuck. Crawl on top of my shoulders." But Hulk's bark sends Red huddling into a ball, burying his head between his legs. My entire body shakes. I feel trapped like when I was stuck in Farmer Frank's root cellar during the storm. It was Brian's common sense that pulled me through that fear.

Common sense, I repeat. Suddenly, I realize I've never been around Hulk long enough to really get to know him. Maybe his gruff voice doesn't really bite. After all, he played along with our water balloon game. He just played in a giant-size way.

I figure I'd rather be crushed by Hulk than grounded by Mom. Either way, I might not survive. So what do I have to lose? I manage to get the wild thump-thump in my chest to slow and my tongue to tame. "I'll get on your shoulders," I say.

Even before I can decide if I made the right decision, Hulk whisks me off the ground and launches me skyward. I quickly grab onto the broom handle. In one motion, Hulk takes two steps back, the broom pops out, and he plops me back on the ground.

My hands shake as I clutch the broom. I raise my chin up a fraction of an inch, hoping it's enough to nod a thank you.

Suddenly, Hulk tips his head back and a deep, rich laugh rings out. "Glad to help," he says in a gruff hee-haw. Then he turns and walks away.

"Thanks," I stutter.

Hulk keeps walking, with his back to us, but he lifts his big paw in the air and then drops it to his side. Hulk's form of a wave.

Sometimes you can say a lot without speaking at all.

Chapter 9

Things That Go Zip, Flop, and Hop

Blackness is all around me. The cool night air feels wet against my face, almost like swimming underwater. The rain shower earlier tonight could not have come at a better time.

Soggy soil squishes around my shoes. I take a step forward in the dark, trip, and tumble to the ground. Now on all fours, I pat around and find exactly what I was hoping for – a log. Squatting, I wedge my fingers under it. Pieces of wet bark crumble away. Instantly, I get a whiff of stinky, moldy old wood. Hooray! The smell of dead rotten wood is the secret ingredient to catch big fat night crawlers.

"Shine the light over here," I call to Brian, who is several feet away.

He swings the flashlight toward the sound of my voice, and I give the log a mighty shove. Just as it rolls over and uncovers the mushy dirt underneath, a long, thick night crawler zips into its hole in the ground.

"Where'd he go?" Brian asks.

"Boy! Was he fast," I say, stunned at the worm's disappearing act.

"Try again," Brian says.

He shines the light onto another log. I push, and it easily rolls in the soggy soil, uncovering another crawler. I grab for this one quickly, but all I get is a handful mud. "Holy cow, he's gone, too," I say.

"Okay, Adam, that does it. We need a different plan of attack," Brian says.

"Yeah, maybe I should hold the flashlight."

"A few minutes ago, you were bragging about your genius worm-catching skills."

It's true. I caught a bunch of night crawlers the other night, and it wasn't even raining. Now with the worms crawling to the wet surface, it should be even easier. I hiss through clenched teeth, wishing I had my own flashlight. Unfortunately, while catching crawlers the other night, I set my flashlight down somewhere and have yet to find it. Mom says she's already bought one flashlight per kid this camping trip and that we'll have to make do.

Now my brother won't share his flashlight. I watch it glow like a super power beam into the blackness here in the woods and huff out a sigh. This would be a perfect time for my Batman thermal night vision goggles. Unfortunately, I forgot to pack them.

But not having Bat-goggles or my own flashlight is just a temporary setback because I suddenly have an idea. "Hey, Brian," I say. "Here's the plan. We'll sneak up on the crawler in total darkness."

"Huh? Are you crazy? We're already in the dark," Brian says.

"Turn off the light," I instruct.

"Why?"

"When you turn off the flashlight, I'll get into position, like this," I say, squatting down and thumping the top of a log. "Before you turn the light back on, I'll give the log a shove and get my hand ready to nab the crawler."

"I get it." Brian flicks off the flashlight.

I flip the log. We wait in total darkness as my hand hovers over the turned-up soil. I hold my breath, not moving. All is silent. Then I nudge Brian's leg and he flips on the light. At that very moment, I plunge my hand into the mushy sand and snag a slimy crawler. Gotcha!

As I clutch the mud-covered crawler, I think about the pleasures of camping life: worms tonight, fish tomorrow.

Earlier today, Mom said we needed fish.

"Great, I love to catch fish. Fried fish is my favorite dinner," I said and licked my lips.

"But the fish aren't for eating," Mom said.

"Huh? How come?"

"It's a special project," she said, with one eyebrow raised for added mystery.

"Wait, I don't get it. What'll we do with the fish if we don't eat them?" I asked, scratching my head.

"That's the surprise," Mom said, not letting her eyebrows give away any more hints. "Just catch some big ones and you'll find out tomorrow."

So tonight, using the wait-and-shine flashlight trick, we catch a bucketful of worms. There's a skip in my step as we head back to camp. Whatever the reason, I'm happy to hunt for slimy night crawlers and go fishing.

"Look at the bait, Mom." I hold up the slimy creatures and reach for the handle of the camper screen door.

"Ah, that's nice. But worms stay outside," Mom says as she peeks out from behind the screen door. "Oh my! Look at those shoes!"

"Just a little mud." I wiggle my feet, but they're caked with so much mud I can hardly see my shoes. Or socks. And thank goodness the camper porch light is dim. Wait till Mom sees the brown mess that's spattered all over my T-shirt, too.

"We'll leave the shoes outside," I say. Turning away from Mom, I whisper to Brian, "Doesn't she know the best time to catch worms is after it rains?"

"Something tells me Mom wouldn't care," Brian says, looking down at his mud-covered shorts. "Besides, worms and slugs and messy laundry aren't her favorite part of camping."

"Remember, no pets inside the Moynihan camper," Mom says. "And that includes the ant farm and that crawly thing in the glass jar." She points to the spider in the homemade bug keeper with holes punched in the tin lid for air. Five-year-old Red swung the hammer on that project so the holes are a bit lop-sided.

"It's time to come in and get ready for bed," Mom says as she steps out of the camper. "I just need a few tools from the van for the fish project tomorrow. I'll be right back."

After slipping off the mud-covered shoes, we head to the camper. Brian steps inside and I'm right behind him. But before I get through the doorway, the ant farm I brought from Dad's house catches my eye. Gosh. I forgot to feed my pets. If I'm quick, I can sneak the ants in and out of the camper before Mom gets back. Quickly, I grab the farm from the picnic table and bring it inside. After opening a cereal box, I drop one corn flake on top of the maze of ant tunnels. Next, I'll need a drop of water. Carefully, I begin to measure the water. And that's when it happens – Brian bumps into me. The cornflake box spins and tips, cereal flings in every direction.

"Hey, what's the big idea?" I snarl.

"You're supposed to be doing that outside," he says. My brother likes to follow the rules, like the one about coloring inside the lines. When I go outside the lines, Brian gets upset with me. He doesn't seem to understand it's okay to be a little loosey-goosey.

"Yeah, but doing it inside is faster," I snap.

"Not anymore." Brian can't resist giving me a hard time, so to make things a little more difficult, he crunches the cereal under his feet.

"Stop that!" I give my brother a powerful shove that knocks him off balance. His arms swing wildly, and one smacks the ant farm. It slams against the metal sink. The plastic farm shatters into pieces. Ants and sand and cereal cover the floor. Oh boy! If I had remembered to feed the ants earlier in the day I wouldn't be in this mess.

My jaw moves, but it's several seconds before any words come out. "Hurry, get the broom," I say.

"Why should I help?" my brother asks.

Gee whiz. Why does he have to be stubborn, now? "You want to go fishing tomorrow, don't you?" I ask.

Brian nods yes.

"Well, you can't go without me," I say, reminding him of Mom's buddy system. "So sweep!" I jam the broom and dustpan into his hands.

Brian pokes at the cereal with the broom.

"Faster! Mom will be coming through that door any second." Gosh darn it, I wish I had more time. Getting down on my knees, I use my hands to push the mess toward Brain. Yikes. I will never be done in time. If wishes could come true, Mom would be back in an hour. Better yet, she wouldn't come back till tomorrow. Tick, tick, tick, seconds race by. My wish doesn't come true, though, and too soon we hear the rattle of the metal door as Mom twists the knob to enter.

"Oh no!" Brian says, staring at the cereal bits still scattered on the floor. His green eyes spin with fear, knowing we're out of time.

"Go out and stop her," I say.

"How?"

"You're smart so think of something brainy!" I push Brian out the screen door.

"Hi, Mom. What are you doing?" I hear Brian squeak. Oh boy, where is Brian's textbook wisdom when I need it? But there's no time to worry about his yammering. Instead, I need to fix this mess. Why don't campers have vacuum cleaners? I wish I had the big shop vacuum like Dad keeps in the garage. That one can suck up even wood chips and scraps from our Cub Scout building projects.

Wildly, my eyes scan the camper. There aren't many choices. I grab the trash bucket, lay it on its side on the floor, use the dustpan as a shovel, and scoop up all the pieces in one big swoosh. My heart sinks as I watch the ants fall into the trash. I fed and watered them the entire school year.

Mom and Brian enter the camper.

"Oh, I was just taking the trash to the dumpster. Then I'm ready for bed," I say.

Not waiting for a reply, I dart out the door and whip around to the backside of the camper with the bag. There is enough light from the window for me to work quietly. I carefully dump the bag. "Here you go little fellows. Have a good life," I whisper to my pet ants. They quickly crawl away into the sandy woods.

I gather up the broken ant farm pieces, put them back in the trash bag and take them to the recycling bin. Super glue can't fix the ant farm, and I don't have enough money in my piggy bank to buy another one.

At times like these, there is comfort in eating something sweet, like an Oreo – or three – so I head to the camper. Once back inside, things are even better than I had hoped. Brian is eating a bedtime snack of chocolate ice cream with hot fudge syrup and whipped cream. And there is a bowl for me.

The next morning, the sun shines brightly and the sky is the color of faded blue jeans – my favorite color. Yes, it's a perfect day to go fishing.

"Catch a big one," Mom says with a sunny smile.

"How many fish do we need?" I ask.

"At least one apiece," she says, still not giving any more hints about the special project. "Are you fishing off the rocks?" she asks.

"Of course," I say. "No more hanging over the safety rail for me."

The Muskegon Lake channel is lined with large boulders that form a waterway to the great Lake Michigan. Until this summer, Mom, Mrs. Safety, said I could only watch the older kids sit on the huge rocks fishing far below. I waited for the day when I would be old enough to go onto the rocks and today is it.

At the channel, Brian and I hop from rock to rock. We find the perfect spot and settle in with the night crawlers and minnow bucket between us. Sitting high on a boulder, I cast out the line of my pole and watch the red and white bobber float on top of the lightly rippling water. I watch and wait.

Soon, the summer sun beats down on us and a trickle of sweat drips down my back. A boat whizzes by, and its wake whips up a wave. It crashes against the rock and sprays a cool mist over us. Even though we've been fishing for more than fifteen minutes without a nibble on the bobber, I still believe this is the best place ever – fishing off the rocks.

"Hey Sweetie. I was looking for you two." Without looking up, I know that voice belongs to Freckles. Before this camping trip, I thought only Great-Aunt Mabel called people Sweetie, but I guess not. Freckles says it all the time.

Brian looks cross-eyed at me. I never told my brother about Freckles and how she helped me with the Halloween costume.

"Can I fish, too?" she asks.

Before we can answer, Freckles plunks down between us and has her own line in the water. I didn't even see her put a night crawler on the hook. Could she be afraid of worms? A couple of days ago, when she and I scouted for sticks for the costume, I thought she might have been scared of snakes. As it turned out, I was the one to bolt first when the big blue racer spit its purple tongue at us. I never did find out if she was afraid of snakes.

"Hey! I got one," she says as her bobber sinks and pole bends. She gives the pole a quick jerk and reels in a big bluegill, its pale yellow belly shining in the sun.

"Now what do I do?" she asks.

Brian's eyes meet mine, green on green. How can Freckles snag a fish in less than a minute and not know what to do next?

"Haven't you ever caught a fish before?" I ask.

"Heck no. Sweetie, this is my first time on the rocks. Don't you love it?"

The fish flips and flops on the rocks, so I grab it and release the hook. But what is this? A mini rubber worm comes out of the fish's mouth.

"You're using a lure?" I ask.

"Isn't it pretty? It's purple!" she says.

"But purple worms are for cloudy lakes," Brian says. "In clear water like this, you're supposed to use green worms."

"Yeah, but the purple worm did catch a fish," she says. "Probably because it matched my dress."

She's wearing her usual camp outfit, a froufrou dress fit for a princess. And today, she has so many barrettes in her hair she looks like a display rack in a store.

I shake my head. Brian shrugs his shoulders as he slips the bluegill into the minnow bucket for Freckles. Getting back to fishing, I settle onto a big boulder and watch my bobber. Soon, I feel a tug on the line. A-ha. I got one – and with a big, ugly night crawler as bait. Brian gets lucky, too.

"I think my fish is the biggest," Freckles says. "But I won't tell anyone, ever. Pinky swear." She holds up her little finger.

"Let's measure the fish." My brother is quick to get to the truth.

We hop off the rocks and dump the fish out onto the sand. I lay my fish next to theirs, but it's hard to measure.

"It won't hold still. It's slipping through my hands." I try to hold onto the wet and scaly fish, but it escapes, flipping and flopping in the sand.

"It's heading toward the water!" Brian shouts.

We scramble after the runaway fish.

"I got it!" Freckles says as she scoops up the wiggly escapee.

Brian lifts the lid of the minnow bucket, and she slips in my pride and joy.

"That was a close call," I say.

"Let's head back to camp," Brian says, picking up the bucket.

"What are you doing with the fish?" Freckles asks.

"My mom is planning a project," I say.

"Ooo-la-la, your mom is an artist. I can't wait to see what we're going to do," Freckles says.

Did she say *we*?

"Oh, darn," Brian mouths to me.

"Come on," Freckles says, starting to run ahead.

"Hey, wait!" I try to catch up but stumble over my fishing pole and the night crawlers go sailing, spilling out of the container.

"Clear out of the way," Brian says from behind.

But it's too late. He trips over the tangled fishing line. Worms squirm and flee in every direction. My hands can't grab them fast enough.

"Adam, you're getting mostly sand," Brian says.

"Then help me." The tangled fish line is now mixed with the wiggly worms.

"Ah, just let the worms go," Brian says. "We need to get back to camp."

By the time Brian and I gather the gear and reach the campsite, Freckles is helping Mom set out supplies. I wish Mom wasn't so friendly. I can tell Freckles is here to stay.

On the picnic table are paint trays filled to the brim with different colors. Mom said there wouldn't be fish to eat for dinner, but fish and paint confuse me.

Then Brian holds up a white T-shirt from the stack on the table. "What are the shirts for?" he asks.

"We're going to paint the fish, then print it onto the T-shirt," Mom says. "It's called a transfer image."

"So the fish will be painted here?" I ask and thump my chest.

Mom nods yes.

"Oh, how lovely," Freckles says. "We'll be wearing the fish instead of eating them."

"That's right," Mom says. "We won't have to clean the fish like when we cook them for dinner. All we have to do is cover them with paint and press."

This sounds fun. On paper, I like to paint big green dinosaurs with yellow teeth that snap at the sky. A fish I can wear on a T-shirt will be even better than dinosaurs.

We gather around the table. Eager to get started, Brian and I plop down and lean forward, elbows on the table. But Freckles is perched upright, with her hands folded neatly in her lap.

"Would you like a paint smock to cover your beautiful dress?" Mom asks Freckles.

"Mom, those are her play clothes," I say and roll my eyes.

Freckles nods her head, agreeing with me.

"I'll go first," Brian says and grabs a paintbrush. The fish are quiet now, no longer flopping about. He dabs a rainbow of colors across his fish.

"Now, pick up your fish and flip it over onto the front of your T-shirt," Mom says.

Brian clutches his colorful fish and presses it onto the front of the T-shirt. Then, he lifts it off.

"Look, it makes an exact image of the fish," Freckles says.

"And it's lying perfectly in the middle," I say. "It's flawless."

"Like my sister," Freckles whispers to me with a little giggle.

I smirk, too, thinking about the similarities between Freckles' sister and my brother. For instance, on a sunny day, they'd both choose to stay inside, doing something like mixing table salt and shampoo to discover DNA from bananas. Unlike me, I'd rather play outside.

"Who's next?" Mom asks.

"I'll go," I say, dipping a brush into the yellow paint and spreading it across the fish. I smear on blue next, and the colors mix to make green. "Okay, here we go." I shove up my shirtsleeves and grasp the fish.

"Maybe you put on too much paint," Brian says as he sees globs of it squish through my fingers.

"Oops." I try to hold the fish steady. But it's wet and really slimy.

"I can help," Freckles says and reaches across the table with dry hands.

"No, wait! The fish is slipping!" I cry out.

It's too late. Freckles bumps me and the fish flies out of my hands. It flips and lands on the front of the T-shirt. And I do, too. My paint-covered hand is smack dab on the shirt next to the fish. I peel off my hand and then pick up the fish.

At first I'm upset. I wanted my T-shirt to look like Brian's perfect shirt.

But then I hear what Freckles thinks about my shirt. "The hand that caught the fish!"

She's right, I realize, breaking into a grin. On the T-shirt, glowing in blue, green, and yellow, is a one-of-a-kind image of my cockeyed fish and my open-palm hand.

"Your turn, Freckles," I say while wiping my hands with a towel.

Freckles looks at her fish. But she doesn't start painting it. Instead, she paints her hands.

"What are you doing?" Brian asks. We both wonder why she is making such a mess, painting her hands and not the fish.

"Watch this." She plops her hands onto the front of her T-shirt. "These are the helping hands."

I chuckle. This girl is a bit like me after all. She mixes things up.

Freckles is called to lunch, so she thanks us and heads back to her campsite with her T-shirt, her fish, and her pole with the purple rubber worm.

I'm so happy about my fish painted T-shirt I say to Brian, "Let's make Mom a shirt."

He nods in agreement and adds, "It'd be great if we could catch a bigger fish for her T-shirt."

We grab a quick lunch and leave to fish off the rocks.

"Should we to hike to Lake Michigan harbor?" I ask, thinking about another fishing spot.

"It's a longer walk, but it's less crowded with people. I bet we'd catch bigger fish there," Brian says.

We pass our earlier fishing spot and wander toward the end of the channel break wall. We stop halfway to climb down its rocky edge, and then stroll along the sandy shoreline. We head for the jumble of rocks that form the opposite side of the harbor. Muskegon State Park harbor is a safe place for boats. During a storm, big Lake Michigan can kick into a wild rage of powerful waves, but the harbor offers safety when the weather turns ugly.

Along the way to the north break wall, there is a small sand dune to climb. Hiking up the dune, the hot sand squeaks under our feet. Suddenly, out of the corner of my eye, I spot a dark speck jumping in the sand.

"What was that?" I ask.

"It went that way," Brian says.

"No, over this way." I point in the opposite direction.

Brian heads one way, and I explore the other, chasing the jumping action into a clump of tall dune grass.

"I caught it!" he calls.

Rushing over, I peek at the brown spec in his cupped hands. It's a tiny sand toad, just a bit bigger than a nickel.

"Hey, the minnow bucket will make a great toad-catching container," Brian says.

"Yeah, it has a lid." I grab the bucket and lift the lid just a sliver. Plunk, Brian slips the toad inside and I snap it shut. Ping, ping, the toad jumps against the metal bucket.

The fishing poles lie idle in the sand. Mom's fish T-shirt will have to wait.

"Over here, Adam," Brian calls.

"No, wait, one jumped this way." I spin in a circle.

Tiny toads hop every which way. I try to follow their path, but their crazy jumps make my head move side-to-side faster than a Ping-Pong ball during a table tennis tournament.

Through the dune grass, I try to track them. I creep close to the ground, my nose almost touching the sand. Spotting one, I cup my hand and scoop. But the bouncy little guy is quick. It springs up, kisses my cheek, and leaps away. I look at my hand. Whew. It's not green. For a second there, I was worried I'd turn into a frog.

It takes many more scoops to catch a toad, but it's worth the effort. The little critter tickles in my cupped hands and makes me giggle. Thoughts of Mom's fish T-shirt are long gone.

"I've caught another. That makes five for me," Brian says. "Hey, look, the toads like the coolness of the shadows. And watch, sometimes they dig backwards to bury themselves into the cooler sand."

How can Brian see all that? All I see is crazy jumping. These springy little guys are real circus acrobats, bouncing like the sand is a trampoline.

"I caught a whole family," Brian says. "This makes twelve. Let's head home."

Boy, I wish I had big hands like Brian's.

The minnow bucket pings as we stroll up to the campsite.

"What's that sound?" Mom asks.

"Look." I hold out the minnow bucket. "They're tiny sand toads."

Mom squints and wrinkles her nose as I lift the lid, just an inch. "Oh my, aren't they cute," she says. "Just remember, pets stay outside."

I empty a firewood box and turn it upside down to form a cage. Brian adds a small bowl of water for drinking, and it becomes a perfect toad house. "Toads like to eat bugs and insects that are alive, so we should let them go every day," Brian says.

"That's great, then we'll just catch another bucketful," I say.

Each morning, we hike along the secret path carrying the minnow bucket but no fishing poles, which means Mom never got a fish-print T-shirt. Instead, I sneak in the shadows of the dune grass and try to catch springy sand toads. I get lucky now and then, but most of the time I just get sand.

Meanwhile, Brian rules. "I've caught fifteen," he chimes.

How does he do it so fast? The minnow bucket in his hand pings and his flawless fish-print T-shirt doesn't have a speck of dirt on it. The truth is, sometimes I wish for things that can't be, like being more like Brian. Wiping

my grubby hands on my T-shirt, I catch sight of the
cockeyed fish and brightly colored hand print splattered
across it. Sometimes, I'm glad my wish doesn't come
true. It's fun to be me, Adam Moynihan, doing things the
Adam Moynihan way.

Chapter 10

Full Speed Ahead

I see sand.

I see Caleb.

I see trouble.

And it's coming this way.

Caleb, my friend Red's cousin, storms into our campsite. Everywhere Caleb goes, he blows in like a tornado. Arms whirl, feet spin, dust rises – a real sandstorm of a kid.

Hurriedly I swing my arms and legs across Hole No. 6, trying to protect the "water trap," which is an empty Cool Whip container buried in the sand and filled with water. All morning I've shoveled and scraped sand to make a crazy mini-golf course that snakes through the entire campsite. It's an Adam Moynihan masterpiece. Okay, Brian helped, too.

Then Caleb blasts toward me. "Holy Cow! What're you guys making with all the sand pails and wood? Can I help? I love to build. What can I do? Is there an extra shovel for me?"

Caleb may be my size, but his bulldozer movements and big booming voice make my hair stand on end.

I haven't played with Caleb since Brian and I built a wooden jail. Caleb was explosive. On that project, his first step, which was more of a soaring, soccer-like kick, knocked over the bucket of nails and they skyrocketed. Then, instead of just picking up each nail, Caleb scooped them up, steam shovel-style, mixing sand and nails into one heaping mess. After that, he plowed into Brian's neatly stacked stash of lumber. Lucky for us, Caleb got called home soon after.

But now, "The Tornado" is back among us. "So what are you building? Why all the sand? Where did all the wood come from?" he chatters.

I silently hope he wanders away.

"We're using some of the lumber left over from the last project," Brian says, carefully smoothing the sand to level the bridge on Hole No. 7. My brother has a lot more patience than I do. He can even wait for just-baked cookies to cool so he doesn't burn his tongue. Me? I toast my tongue every time.

Running at full speed, Caleb darts in a circle around the mini golf course. This kid is a train wreck waiting to happen. "Wow! This is great. I can help. I can hold the wood. Or should I dig a hole? Unless you want me to shovel and hold? Or maybe I could help with the bridge. I love bridges."

"Caleb, slow down!" I snap. "Brian's good with the bridge," I say, through clenched teeth. When Caleb is around, I have no control over the words that come out of my mouth. Thank goodness Brian is calm.

"Come here, Caleb," Brian says. "Just hold the wood steady for the bridge. Nice and steady." Caleb wiggles and squirms. "Easy does it. Don't move," Brian says as he puts his hand over Caleb's jet-propelled fingers.

"I'll grab paper to make the flags," I say and head toward the camper. It's either that or put a sock in my mouth to keep from slinging zingers at Caleb. I hop up the two-step entrance, and from the kitchen drawer, I snag scissors, paper, and a marker.

"I see you're building, again," Mom says. "It looks like one of your sandcastles at the beach."

"It's bigger and better than castles," I brag. In fact, it's the years of making sandcastles that gave us the idea.

"Is it a sand maze?" Mom asks.

"Nope," I say. "But I'll give you a hint. We used wood."

"A racetrack?"

"Nope."

"Hmm, I'd better take a closer look." Mom heads outside. I'm at her heels.

"Take this, Mom," I say and place a putter in her hand that I got from her golf bag earlier.

"Oh, it's a putt-putt course. How fun!" She steps up to the first hole.

Earlier, in our camping vacation, Brian and I found leftover pieces of two-by-fours. Using that same treasure pile of wood, we've built a ladder, a tent, a hideout, raft, dock, jail – and now a goofy golf course.

Hole No. 1 is a small rock wrapped in duct tape hanging from a tree branch with dental floss. The rock drops over a hole we dug in the sand.

"Stand here, Mom. Aim for the hole." I center her feet.

Then I jog several steps to the hole and give the rock a light tap. The rock swings like a pendulum that gets in and out of the path of the putter's ball.

"Make sure the rock isn't in the way. It's all about timing, Mom," Brian says.

"Timing?" Mom asks as she squints and leans toward the hole. "There's not much time to sink the ball."

"Hey guys, I can fix that." Before we can blink, Caleb jumps up and gives the rock a mighty swing. "Oops. I pushed it too hard. Maybe the rock should be like this, I could slow it down, unless you want the rock to go in a circle. I could - -"

"Right there is fine, Caleb," Mom says. "Step away and I'll swing." She tightens her grip and shifts her feet in the sand. Then she wiggles her hips like she is doing a dippy dance. Her shoulder-length brown hair swishes in time to the rhythm in her head. Jeez, moms can be so embarrassing. Finally, she stops wiggling and swings. The ball rolls along in the sand, but stops short of the rock and target hole.

"Hey, look at that gizmo over there," Caleb says and darts to a different hole.

Cripes, we haven't even finished the first hole and Caleb yanks out the empty can we buried for the tunnel hole. Sand explodes and dust rises. In seconds, Caleb has his hand inside the empty can that Brian cut the top and bottom out of. The can jiggles on his wrist like one of Mom's bracelets. Caleb has destroyed the tunnel hole faster than the speed of light. Then something worse happens.

Caleb races to Hole No. 3 – The Trench. It's the best trick on the course. Brian and I carved the trench to slope downward and then filled it with pebbles the size of jellybeans. We planned for the golf ball to roll gently down the trench and lose speed. That is, until now. Instead of slowly swinging a golf club, Caleb fires golf balls like he is a baseball player hurling fastballs. Pebbles fly every which way. The Trench will be destroyed in seconds. I can't watch. I cover my face with my hands.

"Let's play with a golf club," Brian says. I peek through my fingers as Brian gently takes Caleb's hand. Next, Brian slowly leans closer to Caleb and whispers in his ear, "Do you know the secret of golf?"

Caleb shakes his head no.

"The secret is to play it in slow motion. Very ... very ... slow ... motion," Brian says.

Brian's mild manners remind me of Clark Kent. And my brother's charm has the power of Superman, too. For the first time today, Caleb stands still.

Afraid this moment won't last, I step in with an idea of my own. "Okay, Caleb, I'm turning the magic key on your back and everything you do will be in slow motion."

"I get it!" Caleb says, "I'll move like a turtle, or a snail, or should I be a slug?"

To my surprise, we get Caleb to slow down and we play a couple of holes together. Then, luckily, he gets called to lunch.

"I'll make lunch, too," Mom says.

"Wait, Mom. Stay and play another hole," I say. "It's the teeter-totter hole."

"Swing hard enough for the ball to roll up this slope." Brian taps the tilted board. "Then the board will tip from the weight of the ball." Brian's hand shows the teeter-totter effect.

Mom aims. Clunk. The ball hits the wood. It lies in the sand like a dead fish, not moving.

"That's a Mulligan, a golfing term for a bad shot. It means you get to do it over and not keep score," I say. "Swing again."

"This is fun," Mom says. "In fact, I think you boys are ready for a real golf course."

"And play with clubs like yours?" I ask. Mom's golf bag holds more clubs than Tiger Woods' bag of thirteen.

"That set of clubs in the van is an old one of Grandma Barb's," Mom says. "I don't play much golf, even though Grandma would like me to."

Not play much? I have never known Mom to play golf. I wonder if she even knows the rules. Then she winks. That wink tells me Mom knows Mother Magic – something Mom knows that I think she doesn't. For instance, she can rattle off who won the World

Series for the past three years without ever watching a baseball game.

"You boys can play tomorrow, first thing in the morning. There won't be so many people on the course," Mom says. "We'll go to Hickory Knoll."

"Why Hickory Knoll and not Lincoln Golf course?" Brian asks as he names one of Michigan's top-rated courses Dad has talked about.

"Hickory Knoll has a 'white course' called a Par 3. The holes are shorter and easier to learn," she says, giving grown-up reasons why it is the best course for us kids.

My head drops and shoulders sag at the idea of a short course. Par 3 seems like a Happy Meal when I had my heart set on a Big Mac.

"If you do well on this course, maybe we can take you to play the island hole Pete Dye designed at Eagle Eye Golf Course in East Lansing," Mom says.

Pete Dye! My head lifts up and my eyes grow to the size of golf balls. Pete Dye is the greatest architect of golf course design. My friend, Lucas, from Lake Hills School, boasts that he and his Dad have played Eagle Eye. Mom knowing about Eagle Eye is Mother Magic at its best.

"There is one thing before golf tomorrow," Mom says softly. So softly, I almost don't hear her.

Uh-oh, Mom has a twist. But, that's okay. Nothing can spoil the thrill of playing on a grown-up golf course, even if it is a Par 3. Hickory Knoll is simply a hurdle to jump before I play the great Pete Dye's island hole.

"What do we have to do before we can play golf?" I ask.

"I think you should earn the money to play," she says.

"How?" I ask.

"Well, Caleb's Mom would like you to babysit Lilly while she takes Caleb into town," Mom says.

"Sure, that's great," Brian says.

I nod in agreement. Easy money, I think. How hard can it be to watch a three-year-old for a couple of hours? Especially since Caleb won't be around. Maybe we can babysit another time, too, so we can earn even more money! Then I can buy athletic shoes with a brand name the kids at school will drool over. And a computer for my own room, too. As we head in for lunch, my mind is a whirlwind, dreaming about all the things I'll be able to buy.

Drying the last lunch dish, I see a white van pull up to the campsite. Caleb rides co-pilot next to his mom. Brian and I dart from the camper, ready to earn our easy money.

Caleb's mom gets out of the van and opens the side door to unhook Lilly out of her car seat. At the same time, she introduces Lilly to us and then gives us a few instructions. All the while, Caleb swings and sways in his seat as if the radio is on. But no music plays. I wonder if this kid ever sits still.

Once unfastened, Lilly jumps out of the van and I grab her hand. She has a head full of bouncy brown curls that spring in every direction as she rocks in her shoes. As soon as the van is out of sight, Lilly escapes my grip. She bolts to the putt-putt course and beelines to the Cool Whip container filled with water. Instantly she tosses in pebbles, sticks, sand, and anything else within her reach.

That's when I realize that Lilly is a bit like Caleb.

"Slow down, Lilly," Brian says and takes her hand. "Let's make this a game. Let's guess if the item you toss in the water will sink or swim."

My brother's idea is brilliant.

"Like this." I hold up a plastic pop bottle cap. Lilly watches as I twirl the cap between my fingers like it's part of a magic act.

"I think the cap will swim and float on top of the water," Brian says.

"I think the cap will …," I say, hesitating on purpose to keep the magic alive. Slowly I wave the cap 'round and 'round over the water. "I think the cap will sink! What do you think, Lilly?"

"Sink, sink, sink!" She claps her hands and jumps in place.

I toss the cap into the water. Plop. Ripples of water swirl around the cap. Lilly giggles as we all stare at the cap floating in the water.

"More, more. Let's play more, more, more!" Lilly yips like a playful puppy and spins in a circle.

I dash into the camper and grab whatever I can find to keep Lilly busy.

Back outside, I ask, "How about a pencil?"

"Sink, sink, sink," she says and hops about. I toss in the pencil.

"Tee hee," Lilly laughs as the pencil floats. "More, more, more."

Not even a magician could keep up with Lilly. Since I can't pull a rabbit out of my hat, I pull out the next item I'd snatched in the camper. "How about a pickle? Does it sink or swim," I ask.

"Swim, swim, swim." Lilly yaps nonstop. Her brown curls spring like a Slinky as she bounces around the Cool Whip container.

In a flash, we test a spoon, paper clip, safety pin, button, toothpick, 9-volt battery, rubber band, and Mom's nail file.

The game keeps Lilly busy for ten minutes. Now we need to figure out a plan for the next hour and fifty minutes.

"Close your eyes, Lilly," Brian says, quickly digging a small hole in the sand and burying a spoon.

I understand Brian's game and cover Lilly's eyes with my hands. "Don't peek, he's not quite finished."

As fast as he can, Brian shovels and piles sand until there are three little mounds. Lilly wiggles and squirms, trying to sneak a peek. I hold on tight to keep her eyes covered. Finally, after what feels like ten minutes, I let my hands fall from her face and say, "Open your eyes, Lilly."

"In which pile is the spoon buried?" Brian asks.

In a split second, Lilly points and says, "This one." She swishes her hand across her first choice. Sand flies and I cough on the dust as Lilly uncovers the spoon.

She laughs and wants to play again. We dig, giggle, hide, and laugh as we cover and uncover the spoon. Fifteen more minutes go by.

"Now what?" I ask Brian.

"What do you mean, Adam? I came up with 'Sink or Swim' and the 'Spoon Guessing Game.'"

"You've got brain power," I say.

"Yes, but we're supposed to be babysitting *together*," Brian snaps back, arms folded across his chest. "Now, it's your turn, little brother, so try to think of something." I hear his breath wheeze through pressed lips as he snarls out a sigh. A rush of his hot air hits me in the face.

It's rare for my brother to lose patience, but sometimes, he's just like me.

Think, Adam, think, I say to myself. But my mind is blank. Babysitting is harder than I thought. At this rate, we might have to ask Mom for help, and then we won't get paid. No grown-up clubs. No Par 3. No Pete Dye.

Suddenly, I get a face full of sand. It's Lilly. She flings sand with the spoon.

"Hey, hey, don't throw sand," I say as I spit out a mouthful of sand.

That's all it takes. Lilly starts crying. Then she's wailing. The tears pour and she howls so loud it hurts my ears.

"Now look what you did," Brian barks at me.

Her screams are louder than a police siren, and she spins in circles faster than the twirling bubble light on top of a police car.

"Quiet, quiet," I say, but Lilly keeps bawling. "I'm sorry ... uh ... let's play something else."

I try to cuddle her but she swings her arms at me. This is hopeless. The tears and screams are endless, and so loud, my ears ring.

"Hush, hush, shhh ... listen ... do you hear that?" Brian asks in a soft whisper. "Can you hear birds singing?"

It's a miracle. Suddenly, Lilly is silent. My brother's Superman charm happens again.

Working with Brian's bird trick, I gently take Lilly's chubby little hand and put it in mine. Together we point up to the top of an evergreen tree. "Listen for the birds," I repeat my brother's words of wisdom. Lilly's eyes follow my extended finger. "Look up high," I say.

"Pinecone," she says and slaps my hand away. "Me want pinecone."

Perhaps birds aren't the perfect answer.

"Pinecone, pinecone, pinecone." Lilly's chant echoes in my ears. Wait! That's the answer to the problem.

"Hey, Brian, let's have Lilly make a pinecone bird feeder like we did in Cub Scouts," I say.

"With peanut butter and oatmeal?" he asks.

"Yeah, we've got all the supplies," I say. "I'll take Lilly for a walk to collect the pinecones, while you gather the stuff from the kitchen."

Lilly and I pick up pinecones and then meet Brian back at the picnic table.

"Okay, Lilly, here's what we'll do. You'll help pour out sunflower seeds and put them into the bowl," I say.

"Me good cook," she says. "I like to stir."

Brian helps Lilly pour and measure the seeds and oats.

Digging out peanut butter from the jar is a bit stickier. Lilly shoves the entire spoon into the peanut butter jar. Instantly her entire hand is swallowed up in the jar and then she spins and twirls the spoon to scoop peanut butter into the size of a baseball.

Before she can fling a peanut butter fastball, I reach for her arm. "Wait a second, you can lick the lid." I exchange the spoon with the peanut butter blob for the lid.

Luckily, this time Lilly is a good sport. No crying. She takes the lid and licks, while I save the peanut butter blob from becoming a fly ball.

Brian drops a small amount of peanut butter into the oats and seeds. "Okay, Lilly, now we'll mix it all up."

"Like this?" she asks. But before I can hand her a mixing spoon, she thrusts both hands in the bowl, mashing and mixing. Peanut butter, oats, and seeds squish between her fingers.

"Eeeyuw," she says.

The jumbled mess sucks up her small hands. In seconds, she is up to her elbows in sticky peanut butter gunk. She whips her hands 'round and 'round. Wads of sticky goop fly out of the bowl and splatter a mess all over the picnic table and onto the sand, too. Thank goodness we're outside.

"That's enough mixing," I say. "Let's fill the pinecone."

"Like this?" Lilly grabs a pinecone, flings it into the bowl and begins crushing it with her hands.

"No, wait, wait, not so fast," Brain says. "Slow down, gently stuff the pine cone."

"Lilly, watch. It's magic." I use our Caleb slow-motion-trick. "I'm turning a pretend key that makes you move like a turtle."

"Oh, fun. Me slowpoke," she says.

It works. Lilly pats gently and slowly stuffs the pinecone.

Now that the bird feeders are finished, there is one major problem. How to clean Lilly? She has sticky peanut butter goop all over her hands, arms and face. Even on her legs. What a mess.

Let's see, the picnic table can be swept with a broom. That's easy. I wish I could sweep Lilly, too. Maybe we could hose her down at the water spigot where we filled water balloons.

"Come on, Lilly, we're going to clean you up." I reach out to take her hand.

"No, no, no!" She races off.

I chase after her. Suddenly she zooms off in the direction of none other than Hulk. But it's worse than I can imagine. There are two Hulks! And Lilly is headed straight for the bigger one, the one I've never seen before. Could this be his brother? Same wiry brown hair, just taller and broader. Like an army tank with legs.

Lilly keeps running toward them. The Tank spots her heading straight at him. He squats down, and his dark eyes zero in on Lilly. His nostrils flare and he lets out a machine-like rumble. Hulk stands next to him, statue-stiff, stone-faced. Last time I saw Hulk, he helped me with a broom, but right now Hulk is unreadable.

Tank spreads his arms wide open, and Lilly crashes into his powerhouse chest. He wraps his mighty arms around her and launches her high above his head. Then he holds her there, eyes darting rapidly. Lilly hangs on tight, hoisted skyward. I can't see her face, only her brown curls swinging every which way. I try to run to them, but my feet are anchored to the ground.

I pray he won't dropkick her like a football. I'm no longer concerned about the babysitting money. I just want Lilly back, alive.

Knowing I need to act, I hold my hands up in front of me like I'm surrendering at a battle. Please, please, put Lilly gently on the ground, I beg with my eyes. Luckily the corners of Hulk's mouth soften and turn gently upward. This is a big deal, given that Hulk rarely smiles.

"Ease her down. She's a little tyke," Hulk calls out. His deep voice is gruff, but that's better than full throttle.

Slowly, Tank lowers Lilly to the ground. I can't believe what happens next. Tank gives Lilly a tickle in her armpits. She wiggles, giggles, and then skips over to me with an ear-to-ear grin, like she'd been on her favorite amusement park ride. I take her hand and nod to the two giants.

Tank looks at Hulk. They blink once at each other and then turn to me. Together they give me a thumbs up.

I'm glad they're guys of few words because I don't know what to say to them. Instead, I smile as big as a birthday balloon ready to pop, deciding giants can make nice friends. Tank and Hulk lumber away.

By the time I get Lilly to the water spigot, clean her up, and take her back to the campsite, Caleb's Mom drives into the campsite. Whew. I doubt I could survive any more babysitting. I don't relax until I see both Lilly and Caleb fastened in their seatbelts. They bounce up and down like pogo sticks as the white van pulls away from the campsite. I think if it were an electric car, it wouldn't need a battery. Caleb and Lilly generate more than enough energy.

The next morning, I am relieved not to have had nightmares about babysitting. I get dressed and put the money I earned in my pocket. It jingles with every step. After gulping down breakfast, I help with cleanup. I can't wait to play a grown-up golf course, even a Par 3 one. I am certain my first time at golf will go better than my first time at babysitting.

Brian, Mom, and I pile in the van. The curvy, tree-lined road that leads out of Muskegon State Park seems long when we drive to town for groceries, but now it seems even longer on our way to the course. We pass Farmer Frank's cornfield and head farther north. Even with Mom rattling off golf pointers, I squirm in my seat, hoping the course is around the next corner. We pass miles of trees and a few buildings scattered here and there. After Elm and Oak streets, we take a turn, and that's when acres of short green grass appear. Mom calls it a Par 3, but to me, the lush rolling hills go on forever, longer than three football fields. Tiny white flags mark the holes.

Mom pulls into the parking lot. Brian and I bolt out of the van and race to the small clubhouse nearby.

"You look ready to play," a man says sporting a cap with a high-class logo on it – HK – for Hickory Knoll.

Brian and I nod our heads, speechless.

"These clubs are just your size. They're called youth clubs." The attendant hands us each a bag brimful with shiny clubs. We snatch them and sprint to the starting area outside the clubhouse. In a split second, I have the big fat wood driver out.

"Tee up, Adam," Brian says, handing me a toothpick-size piece of wood known as a golf tee.

I step up to a small area of short-trimmed grass and stand between a chunky pair of four inch white cubes. I press the tee into the soft grass and then place a ball on top.

"Place your left hand over your right little finger on the club shaft and then squeeze tightly, like Mom said," Brain instructs.

Squeezing the club, I spread my feet apart in front of the plate – oops, I forgot. This isn't baseball. In golf, it's called a tee box. Everything is so new. It's fun playing like a grown-up. I raise the club over my shoulder and swing down and forward, whacking the ball. It sails through the air and becomes a dot in the sky. Then I see it hit the ground and bounce along the green carpet landing halfway to the first flag. It feels like I hit a grand slam.

Brian tees up and hits his ball. It's a good shot, too, landing close to mine. I yank my very own bag of clubs and heave it onto my shoulder. The weight makes me sway and stagger a bit. But I fix my wobble and am ready to rush ahead. That's when I look over my shoulder and see my brother. Brian is carefully writing our names on the official scorecard, the way he does in every game we play.

"Come on, Brian," I call out, eager to race to the ball and swing again. "You're wasting time!"

I can't believe it. Brian tosses the scorecard in the trash. He just threw away the rules of golf! He's too excited to take the time to keep score. Moving at warp speed we fly to find our balls.

In the distance we hear Mom yell from the clubhouse, "Wait for me!" She hasn't had a chance to pay with the babysitting money we gave her. The attendant is still ringing up the bill.

I wave at Mom and then bolt to where my ball lies. I recall the types of clubs Mom taught me and whip out a shiny silver one. This one is known as an iron, and I pick No. 6 to get the ball into the air. Mom said an air ball will plunk down and stay put rather than rolling out of control. I want this shot to plop down right near the flag. I swing, and the ball soars, dropping down in front of the first hole.

Brian swings. Like me, he hit a good shot and is close to the flag.

I look back. Mom is still in the clubhouse as she waits for her change. "We're heading for the green!" I yell to her, naming the short grass around the flag.

To chase after the ball, I swing the heavy golf bag onto my shoulder. It sways to one side, making me stumble, but it doesn't slow me down. I zip ahead, running like a hunchback all the way.

On the green, we pull out putters. I take two taps and the ball rolls, dropping into the hole, called a cup. Brian taps his ball, and he's in the cup, too. We gather our balls and sprint to tee box No. 2. Using our drivers, we whack the ball down the long, green lawn known as the fairway. Mom finally catches up. She doesn't carry her golf bag.

"Where are your clubs?" I ask.

Mom gasps for breath. "If I golf, I won't be able to keep up with you. It's easier to be a spectator today."

My first time on a grown-up course is a hit. Especially, since we aren't keeping score. Brian and I speed ahead. Only a few trees and weeds in the rough slow us down. In fact, we move almost as fast as Caleb and Lilly.

Chapter 11

Mountain Size Whoppers

A coin spins and flips in the air. There is a fifty-fifty chance I could win this. Within seconds, the prize might be mine.

"Heads!" I call.

"Tails!" Brian says while we watch the quarter flip.

It lands in the sand between our bare feet. We huddle close, hovering over the coin to read the imprint. George Washington looks up at me.

"Hooray! It's heads," I say. Being the winner means I get to pick the next activity.

The beach gang – Mom, Grandma, Brian, and me – are at Lake Michigan. We've just finished swimming to cool off from the August heat while Papa is back at camp cooling off in his own favorite way – in a lawn chair under a shady oak, watching the boats motor in and out of the channel. That sweet spot by the channel is why Campsite No. 21 is his favorite.

Without hesitation I grab Grandma's hand and pull her closer to me ready to reveal my winning choice.

"What are we going to do?" Grandma asks.

"Here's the plan," I say. "Brian and Mom will drive the van back to the campsite. We're taking the shortcut up that sand dune," I say, pointing away from the water to the large row of rolling sand dunes that stretch along the shoreline.

"Are you sure it's a shortcut?" she asks.

"Of course it is. All we have to do is climb up that hill. The camper will be on the backside."

Actually, I wasn't certain about the shortcut. It was a guess because I have never hiked the sand dunes from the beach to the campground before. But I figure the sand-dune route shouldn't take much longer than the five-minute car ride. Besides, I have an uncommon amount of curiosity.

"Will this be another Adam Moynihan adventure?" Grandma asks.

Just yesterday, I promised Grandma we would share a sundae, even-steven. I ordered a Tommy Turtle, the biggest sundae pictured on the outside walk up window. With spoons ready we dove into the incredible ice cream treat. Instantly, I heard Grandma's false teeth go click, click, click. And her jaw jumped in tiny jerks. Turns out the Tommy Turtle was jam-packed with nuts! The last time Grandma tried to chomp on nuts, her dentures had to go to the dentist for repair. Ever since, it's no nuts for Grandma. So she set her spoon down. It was her last bite, while I got to finish the whole sundae.

"Grandma, when I ordered the sundae, I didn't know it'd have nuts," I say. "I'm really sorry."

She leans forward, scrunches her face, puckering her mouth like yesterday. Then she clicks her teeth at me and we both laugh. Wanting to please Grandma, I say, "You can trust me today. It'll be an easy walk. I promise."

Loading the van with beach gear, I notice my shorts and T-shirt tossed aside from when I changed my clothes before swimming. We usually wear our bathing suits to the beach, but earlier, I was off betting on how high a grasshopper could jump, and completely forgot about swimming. By the time I heard Mom's call, I was late. Really late. I had to change into my bathing suit at Lake Michigan.

Brian and Mom drive back to the campsite. Grandma and I wave good-bye as the van rolls out of sight.

"We just go up this hill," I say, leading her up a sandy path.

A cool breeze sails across Lake Michigan and gently blows against our backs. We also hear the soothing sound of waves behind us on the shore.

On the way up the hill, I snatch a blade of dune grass. "Watch, we can call for wild animals." I press my lips into the blade of grass between cupped hands. Whirr. It whistles a high-pitched sound.

"I tried to do that when I was a kid," Grandma says. "But all I got was a bunch of spit."

I hoot with laughter and then toot on the grass once more, but this time it sounds like a fart. Now, we howl together.

199

The sand dune slope gets steeper. In fact, it's so steep our feet slip in the fine sand. I hold Grandma's hand to help balance her footing. "Just to the top of this bluff," I say.

"By that row of trees?" she asks.

"That's it, not much farther." The sandy path gets narrower and the waist-high dune grass gets thicker all around us.

"Listen, I hear a whip-poor-will." I point toward the tall trees. "Don't you think it's silly the bird's song is the same as its name?"

But Grandma doesn't answer. Instead, she takes off her straw sun hat and fans herself. "Whew, it's hotter up here, away from the water," she says.

"Yeah. It was cooler where we could hear the seagulls squawk along the beach." Maybe if I agree with Grandma, she'll smile again. Instead she licks her lips and waves her hat double-time in an effort to cool off.

"Hey! Look at all these butterflies. They like the hot sun. This is fun, Grandma." I twirl in the open sand dune and swish my arms between the hundreds of fluttering yellow butterflies. "I feel like Yoda with a light saber."

"What do a yo-yo and lifesavers have to do with butterflies?" Grandma asks. Oh boy. Maybe the heat is affecting her hearing.

Taking a few steps, I put my arms around Grandma, "Don't you think hiking is a lot more fun than driving back to the campsite?"

"Well, maybe," Grandma says with hesitation. "But I bet your mom and Brian are already sipping an ice cold root beer." She waves her hat one last swish before she puts it back on her head.

I skip ahead, but I go too fast. Grandma is quite a ways behind. While waiting, I pick up small stones and feathers and things. My jam-packed bathing suit pocket tells me I've been here a while. Grandma finally catches up. Her face is bright red and she takes in big puffs of air.

"Do you need to rest?"

"Just for a minute," Grandma says as she plunks down on a huge rock.

To pass the time, I walk heel to toe around the big rock so it takes me twice as long, giving Grandma time to catch her breath. Behind us, Lake Michigan looks like a big ocean, the color of cornflower blue, my favorite Crayola Crayon color. I hear a dove's coo in the trees ahead. Or is it an owl's hoot? Jeepers, there is so much left to explore.

"Do you feel rested now?" I ask.

Grandma smiles and pulls herself up. "That feels better," she says.

But the slope is steep. With each step, we slip in the sand. In minutes, Grandma is huffing and puffing, again. By now, I realize my instincts were wrong about this easy hike.

"Do you think we're halfway?" Grandma asks.

I'm not sure. We've been climbing for a long time, but there is no sign of Muskegon South Channel Campground. I can't let Grandma realize this.

"Oh, we must be halfway." I try to sound certain.

Grandma's feet start to shuffle. She's tired, again. What can I do? My eyes dart every direction and then finally land on a dead tree limb. I pick it up and hand it to her. "Here Grandma. Use this as a hiking stick."

With each step, she pokes the stick in the sand. This time, Grandma stays right behind me. But the sandy path becomes even narrower and steeper. Grandma's pace begins to slow. Thick bushes and vines snake their way onto the path. Hopefully it's not poison ivy waiting to attack us. Brian says poison ivy likes shade, so the squiggly vine on the sunlit path is probably harmless. Besides, it doesn't have three leaves. How lucky can we get?

Lucky? The word instantly makes me think of the lucky conch shell Grandma gave me. I carry it with me everywhere I go, but when I filled my bathing suit pocket with treasures, I should have felt the lucky shell. Fearing my worst suspicions, I quickly empty my pocket. No shell.

Panic rises up in my throat like twisted poison ivy vines wrapping around my neck. Without the lucky shell, we may never get home. I should have never told Grandma this is a shortcut.

Grandma's straw hat sags on her head, and with each step her sunglasses slip down a little more on her sweaty nose. She seems older than when we started this hike. "Do you think it's much farther, Adam?" Grandma asks.

What can I do? I have to think of something. "Ah, don't worry Grandma, it'll get easier, I promise." Oh boy, Mom would say I just told a fib to Grandma. A big fib. I want to sink into the sand, but if I plop to the ground, the evil vines may eat me entirely. Instead I take a deep breath and look up.

"Hey, I have an idea," I say, "I'll go ahead and peek over that row of trees."

"Okay, I'll stay here." Grandma leans against a tree and wilts like a flower without water.

Dashing ahead, I hike higher along the narrow path into the dense woods. The sun barely shines through the thick cover of leaves over my head.

I hear a rustling noise in the dense shrubs. Whoosh! At first I think it's the wind, but the bushes move in only one spot. The swishing sound grows louder and wilder. Something is coming this way! What if it's a bear? I try to step back, but there's nowhere to go – only more woods out there. The branch in front of me snaps. I spin, lose my balance, and stumble into thick prickly shrubs.

Suddenly, something leaps out of the bush. It glides through the air, gracefully. A deer. I let out a sigh and watch its white tail vanish into the woods.

Wow! A real deer, just like Bambi. It feels wonderful not to have been eaten by a bear. I breathe easier and begin to crawl out from under the darkness of the thorny bush.

"Adam? Adam? Where are you?" Grandma calls.

"Over here," I respond. "I'm just going around the next curve."

But there is no curve. All of a sudden, the path has ended. In front of me is a wall of green leaves. I can't see the sun because the trees are too dense. I can't hear the waves of Lake Michigan because the surf is too far away. My heart races in my chest. Uncertain of what is ahead, I turn and call back to Grandma, "Just a bit longer."

Trying to avoid the prickly thorn bush, I slowly creep backward, away from the shrub. That's when it happens – my feet go out from under me. I slip and tumble, sliding down a sandy wash-out, feet first, landing at the edge of a steep gully.

"Adam? Adam, can you hear me?" Grandma calls out again.

"Just one more minute," I yell out. Heck, it'll take a minute to just catch my breath and pick off all the twigs and leaves that are stuck to me. Then another minute to figure out what we should do.

I pick myself up and try to brush off my shirt full of clingy sticks. I look around. To my left, away from the steep gully, the woods open into a field of dune grass. I hike into the clearing and realize I've walked a circle. In plain sight, Grandma leans against the tree.

"Hey, Grandma. Over here." I give her a big wave.

"Okay, I'll be right there." Grandma moves toward me as she uses her dead branch as a walking stick.

My heart settles into a quiet beat knowing she won't have to hike in the woods anymore. However, the peaceful feeling doesn't last. I am lost. Totally lost.

What would Brian do? With keen senses, he would look at the sky and use the rules of sun placement. But the sun is directly above my head. How can I tell if it's setting in the west when it's straight above us?

Still unsure, I lick my finger and hold it up into the air. "Checking wind direction, Grandma," I call back to her, trying to sound like I know what I am doing. I promised this would be an easy hike. Grandma will never trust me again. My throat tightens as I tell another fib. I point to the open field. "This way is home."

Grandma nods, I think she's too tired to question my reasoning. It's still unclear if we're going in the right direction. I picture us having to spend the night lost in the dunes, along with visions of that giant bear. Where is the lucky conch shell when I need it? I tell myself to be brave, and if I can't be brave, fake it.

The sun beats down on my head and I sweat under my Detroit Tigers ball cap. I whip off the cap and slap it against the palm of my hand. Until now, it's been my lucky hat, because the day I bought it, the Tigers won their game. Since I'm completely out of choices, I take a chance and rub the hat, pretending it's a magic lamp. Truth is, I could use a genie and three wishes right now.

I take a few more steps and tug the cap back onto my sweaty head. My mouth is hot and dry.

And then I hear it. The beastly caw-caw of squawking birds. Huge, ugly black things with ragged wings and bare heads – buzzards – circle above us. I hope they aren't thinking of us for an afternoon snack. I tug the brim of my cap, wishing it was big enough to hide under.

Another gruff squawk, so loud and piercing it makes me jump. My eyes dart up. Immediately, I know what to do. "Grandma, let's go to that high peak," I say. "We can look down and see where the campground is."

"Oh, my stars. Higher yet?" Grandma asks.

"Well, on second thought, why don't you wait here? I'll go." I rush ahead to the next bluff. Looking down, tiny dots line Muskegon Lake – the smaller lake that sits behind Lake Michigan.

"Grandma, I know where we are, that's Snug Harbor and there ... there's the boat launch," I call out. "We pass the boat launch on our way to town in the van. That means our campground is over this way!"

It looks so far away. The campers look like dollhouse furniture. But I'm determined to get Grandma out of the mess I made.

We follow the tiny dots that scatter the campground. Luckily, it's much easier going down the dune. The steep slope pushes us forward, our feet sliding downhill and plopping us at the front entrance of Loop No. 1.

"Grandma, do you want to take the shortcut through the playground to our campsite?" I slip my hand into hers as we walk along the blacktop path.

"No shortcut this time, Adam," Grandma says and gives my hand a little squeeze.

Her walking stick clicks the hard surface of the blacktop road. There is still a shuffle to her step.

Suddenly Grandma stops. She pulls something out of her pocket. "Well, on the other hand, it'd be faster through the playground, and I've had good luck all day." Grandma twirls the conch shell between her fingers.

"Where did you get that?" I ask eyes glued on the seashell.

"I found the shell in the back of the van. It must have fallen out of your pocket when you were packing your T-shirt and shorts with the beach gear," Grandma says.

"So you've had the conch shell during the entire hike?" I ask Grandma.

"I meant to give it back to you and forgot. When I thought we were lost, I put the shell to my ear. As a kid, I believed shells were lucky. The soothing sound of the ocean instantly relaxed me, letting me focus on a wish. Minutes later, you had us home."

Grandma hands me the shell. I give it a rub, treasuring its lucky powers.

"Through the playground?" I ask.

"Through the playground!" Grandma says and tosses the walking stick aside.

When we stroll into camp, Brian is at the picnic table reading another how-to baseball book.

"What took you so long, Adam?" he asks. "I've read four chapters while you were gone."

Grandma looks at me. She sinks into a lawn chair. Her face is pink, which is better than the bright red it was earlier on top of the sand dune.

"We stopped to see a deer," I say. "It was an easy walk." I glance at Grandma. She doesn't say a word. She just winks at me. I feel lucky to have a secret with Grandma.

Chapter 12

Maybe The Dog Ate It ... Or Not

I dig deep into the back of my special camper cupboard, the spot for all my valuable treasures. My hand sweeps around, feeling a lumpy pouch of marbles, a squishy plastic bag of balloons, a broken fishing bobber ... but no shell.

Getting down on all fours, I stick my face into the cupboard. Needle-like pricks of panic race down my spine as I realize it's not inside.

I grab my backpack on the couch, unzip it, and poke into every corner. No shell! I turn it upside down and dump everything out. A Superman comic book, iPod earbuds, and a slingshot fall onto the floor.

"What's up?" Brian asks, coming in from outside.

I don't answer. My tongue is frozen in fear. I drop the empty backpack and keep searching the camper.

"What are you looking for, Adam?" Brian asks, but I shrug him off again.

With the camper search coming up empty, I run out to the van and frantically check there. On the seat. Under the seat. Then I retrace my steps around the campsite, eyes darting to see if I can spy my lucky shell in the sand.

Yesterday Grandma had found it in the back of the van. She had returned it to me at the end of a wild hike in the dunes. I'm certain the lucky shell kept me from being eaten by a bear. But where is it now?

A cool breeze begins to blow and high clouds chase away the warm sunshine. I get a chill but know it's not from the weather change but from the fear that my good luck charm is gone. Worried that my life could turn miserable without it, I search further, wildly digging through the bag of beach toys.

Mom steps out of the camper and says, "This cooler weather is perfect for picking blueberries."

"Do you think we could ride our bikes to the berry patch this year?" Brian asks.

My head whips out from the inside of the beach tote. My brother's idea is a never-been-done-before brainstorm.

Since building a bike jump, I've been doing tricks on my Magna five-speed mountain bike. But to ride cross country is double thrilling. I can already feel the wind in my face from pedaling at high speed through the back roads.

"That's a great plan!" I say, tossing aside the beach tote, instantly forgetting about the lost shell. "Mom, can we ride our bikes to pick blueberries?"

"You've never ridden that far before," Mom says. I can tell by the sound of her voice that she is filled with doubt. Big doubt.

I need a game plan. Somehow I've got to convince her that biking there is a good idea.

In a casual tone, I make my plea, "The blueberry patch can't be that much farther than Farmer Frank's cornfield. Remember? We drove there lickety-split." I snap my fingers for quick effect.

Framer Frank's fresh sweet corn is one of Mom's favorite summer foods. Hopefully, reminding Mom about the tasty treat will help her warm up to the idea of this long distance bike adventure.

But Mom is rock solid, frozen actually. The weather has gotten cooler, sure, but Mom shouldn't be standing there stiff as Frosty the Snowman.

"It'll be an easy ride," I say and give her a sunny smile.

Just then Grandma Barb and Papa drive up to the campsite. As Grandma steps down from the truck, she asks, "What's easy, Adam?" I feel her curious cat-green eyes on me.

Grandma and I have a secret about "easy." Yesterday, I promised her an easy hike through the sand dunes. But the shortcut from the swimming beach at Lake Michigan to our campsite at Muskegon State Park was more like a wilderness survival test. For Grandma especially, it was a hard, hot hike back to the camper.

"Brian and I want to pedal our bikes to the blueberry patch," I say and turn toward Grandpa. "How far do you think that is, Papa?" I ask, trying to avoid Grandma's question. I hope she won't accidentally slip about our sand dune secret.

"Do you have a map in here?" Brian asks Papa. Mom calls Grandpa "old school" because he plans his trips from wrinkled paper road maps. No GPS or MapQuest on the laptop for him.

Brian fishes through the door panel pocket of the truck and pulls out one of the road maps. He jogs over to the picnic table and flattens out the fan-like folds. "Well, let's see. We start here and go north. Up, up, up. Palmer's blueberry patch is nine-point-nine miles away." Brian rattles off the math as he traces the route with his finger.

"That's an easy bike ride," I say directly to Mom, still trying to melt a small icicle-size path into Mom's frosty state. Using the word "easy" is a risk. Grandma might speak up about the crazy dune hike. I quickly change tactics, "Remember, Mom, I've pedaled to school lots of times on my bike." I cast my eyes at Grandma because she is proud of me when I show responsibility, like riding my bike to school. She winks at me. Whew.

"But, Adam, Lake Hills School is three miles from your Dad's house," Mom says, her voice icy cold.

"Yeah, but I've ridden there and back," I say. "That makes six miles. This will be easy."

"But Adam, you didn't pedal all six miles at one time," Mom says. Boy oh boy. Mom is a tough thaw.

"I've got an idea," Brian says. "Papa can be the backup plan. Adam and I will leave first, giving ourselves a head start. Then, Papa will follow in his truck. That way, if we can't make it all the way to the blueberry patch, Papa can pick us up along the bike path."

"That's a great plan," Mom says, finally melting.

"Let's synchronize watches," Brian says to Papa as he holds his wrist close to Papa's to compare the time.

"I'd like to ride a bike, too," Mom says. Our Mom, Mrs. Safety, figures she should ride along with us to the berry patch. I don't mind. I'm just excited for another adventure.

"Which way are you going?" Mom asks. "North past the Sports Complex Luge Run or east along Snug Harbor?"

"Does it matter?" Papa asks with his nose buried in the map with Brian.

Mom says, "If we ride past the Sports Complex, it'll be fun to hear kids whoop and holler down the luge chute in those wheeled summer carts."

"Yeah, and if we take the luge route we can stop and get ice cream at Ruth Ann's," I say. Can life get any better? A cross-county bike adventure and ice cream all in one day.

"Wait a minute," Brian cautions. "Don't forget the luge route has the killer Block House hill on it."

The Block House sits on top of a 700-foot steep hill. It's a copy of Fort Dearborn, rebuilt after a fire in 1964 using timber from a shipwrecked lake vessel.

"Kids around here say the Block House fort is haunted with the spirits of dead sailors!" I say. Sneaking up behind Mom, at that point, I poke her in the ribs and make her jump.

"That settles it," Mom says. "I can take screaming luge carts and scary ghosts, but I'll never be able to bicycle up a 700-foot hill. We'll take the smooth and quiet Snug Harbor bike path."

"Let's get going," I say. I'm ready to lead the pack on a new journey, even though I won't be getting ice cream. A nine-mile bike trip is a dream come true.

"Not quite yet, Adam. We'll go right after lunch," Mom says. "But, grab your new sweatshirts, boys. It's getting cooler."

New sweatshirt? I stop dead in my tracks, having no idea where my sweatshirt is. I retrace my steps. The last time I wore it was at the playground yesterday after dinner. I got hot and sweaty and took it off there. Mom would not be happy that I left my sweatshirt outside overnight. I quickly come up with a cover story.

"I left my sweatshirt at Caleb's," I say to Mom, hopping on my bike. "I'll be right back." I pedal off toward Caleb's camper, but once out of Mom's eye sight, I take a direct route to the playground. My eyes search the two-story slide. No gray sweatshirt. Next, I hustle to the jungle gym. Nothing. Lastly, I spin the merry-go-round. Empty.

We just bought those sweatshirts in town when we picked out firecrackers. If I lost it already, Mom is going to have my hide. I plunk down in the sand next to my bike. Kids wiggle and giggle as they swing from the monkey bars behind me, but there's no laughter from me.

Who could have taken the sweatshirt? Caleb left shortly after I got to the playground. So, it's not likely he has it. I shift one foot in the sand and uncover a few twigs and pebbles. Then I see it. A tiny seashell. Suddenly, I remember the missing conch shell. Without my lucky charm, I'm jinxed. Losing my sweatshirt is proof that an evil spell has been cast over me.

I climb on my bike and pedal slowly in a circle to let my mind whirl as I watch the front wheel spokes spin. Let's see ... I think through my list of suspects. Freckles was at the playground, but she just wears pink and purple, so there is no way she has it. Hulk was there, too, but the sweatshirt would be way too small for him. I start to sweat even though it's cold enough to wear the sweatshirt I can't find. What am I going to do?

Straight ahead, I see a friend of Freckles' riding a bike. She has black hair and yellow eyeglasses, reminding me of a bumblebee. Hey, now I remember, she was at the playground last night. I pedal after her, even though I don't know her name.

I pull up to her campsite just as Bumblebee Girl goes into the camper. I hear a voice from inside saying, "Ella, I'm glad you're back."

Is her name Ella? If I don't know her name, is this trespassing? My knees shake like when I'm in trouble and sent to the principal's office.

Suddenly, a strange stinky odor comes from the trailer. A lady with tiny wads of aluminum foil wrapped in her hair comes to the door. "Ella, there's someone here to see you," the lady says. The foil on her hair makes it look like she's wearing an intergalactic space helmet.

"Oh. Hi, Adam," Ella says as she comes to the screen door.

Whew. At least Ella knows my name. Maybe she knows where my sweatshirt is, too.

"Um, hi," I say. "I'm looking for a gray hooded sweatshirt I left at the playground last night."

"Oh yeah, I saw Lindsay leave with one in her bicycle basket. She must have thought it was hers. But maybe it's yours," Ella says.

This is the best news I've had since losing my conch shell. If Ella wasn't behind that screen door I would kiss her. Well, probably not. But I'd definitely give her a high-five. "That's great," I say. "Can you show me where Lindsay lives?"

"I can't leave now. I have to help my mom shampoo her hair treatment. Can you wait?" Ella asks.

Are you kidding? I'm supposed to be halfway to the blueberry patch by now. Mom is going to shoot me. "Sorry, I can't wait. I'm in a hurry. Can you tell me Lindsay's campsite number?" I ask.

"I don't know the number," Ella says.

The curse continues to create roadblocks. Where is my lucky conch shell when I need it?

But my luck suddenly changes when the lady in the stinky space helmet speaks. "Don't worry, young man. Their campsite is on Muskegon Lake. It's the one with a sailboat wind sock that you can't miss."

A bubble of hope swells in my chest. And then my heart bursts when Helmet Lady adds, "But Lindsay is leaving sometime today on the ferry."

The Lake Effect Ferry is the high-speed car ferry that runs between the cities of Milwaukee and Muskegon. It can race to Milwaukee in two and half hours. I hope it doesn't leave town as fast.

"Gotta go," I say, pedaling like a madman, afraid my sweatshirt might be on the fast-track to Wisconsin. It'd be an easy mistake for Lindsay to think my sweatshirt was hers, since it's plain gray. Now I wish I'd bought the one with the giant skateboard logo on it. No girl would want to wear that one.

I pedal at top speed to Loop No. 2. Just two or three campsites sit along Muskegon Lake beach, so it shouldn't be too hard to find Lindsay's camper.

Up ahead, a sailboat wind sock dances in the breeze as it hangs from one of the campers. I slam on my brakes. Without coming to a complete stop, I whip off the bike and let it fall into a heap on the sand. No time for a kickstand when my sweatshirt might be leaving the state.

I freeze. The campsite is wrapped up tightly. Doors and windows to the camper are closed shut. Lawn chairs are folded and stacked beside it. The bicycles are tied under a tarp, so I can't see if a sweatshirt happens to be stored in one of the baskets. There is no sign of Lindsay. No sign of anyone. "Now what?" I wonder aloud.

Suddenly a motorcycle carrying two riders rumbles up next to me and sputters to a stop. As they get off the cycle, I notice the driver is tall. Really tall. And his stance is broad. Grandma Barb would say this man wasn't raised on just biscuits and gravy. This guy is lean and mean. As he takes off his helmet, he stares at me and barely blinks. Then he takes a giant step toward me.

I can't move. My feet feel like they're stuck in wet cement.

Then the smaller rider, shorter than me, whips off her helmet. Tufts of rumpled hair spike out every which way.

219

She gives her head a wild shake, suddenly her soft brown hair fluffs around her face. I notice her matching Tootsie Roll-brown eyes. "Adam?" she asks.

I nod, hoping she is as nice as her candy-colored eyes.

"It's okay, Dad. This is Ella's friend," she says to Mr. Motorcycle.

"Lindsay?" I ask.

She nods.

Apparently this is enough conversation for Mr. Motorcycle to decide to lumber away and head to the camper.

Lucky for me, Lindsay hasn't left on the ferry yet. But there's no time to ask about it now. Instead I say, "Did you find a gray sweatshirt at the playground last night?"

"Yeah. As I was leaving, I picked up a sweatshirt near my bike. I had my sweatshirt on and off all day, so I figured it was mine. Come to think of it, I haven't looked at it since." She steps over to the bicycles and reaches under the tarp.

I cross my fingers behind my back, wishing I had my lucky conch shell.

Lindsay snatches a gray fleece wad out of the basket and holds it up. "Hey. You're right. This isn't my sweatshirt. Sorry about that," she says and hands it to me.

A kick-up-your-heels victory dance would be fun, but I know I've been gone a while so I keep it short. "Gee thanks, but I'm really late. I've gotta go." I race off on my bike to get back to camp as fast as possible.

Steering into the campsite, I wave my sweatshirt high in the air. "Got my sweatshirt. "I'm ready to go."

The road map is packed away and my brother and Papa are playing Crazy Eights. "What took you so long?" Brian asks.

"Was I gone long?" I say and grin at Grandma, who then glances at her wristwatch. I can tell she is thinking about our long hike, but she doesn't say a word.

After lunch, we saddle up on the bicycles and hit the South Channel trail toward Lake Michigan. Ba-room! I hear the Muskegon lighthouse foghorn blast, not to warn of fog, but because of rough waves on the Big Lake. The recent cold wind has kicked up a wild rage of Lake Michigan surf.

"Yippee! This is like whizzing down a luge run!" I put my feet up on the handlebars and sail along.

"Yeah, we're lucky the wind is blowing at our backs. It's giving us speed to push us fast," Brian yells as he glides by me.

We zip past the state park beach entrance, leaving Lake Michigan and the mighty wind behind us. Turning right, we pedal east along Memorial Drive.

"Phew, is that you, Brian?" I ask my brother and laugh.

"Not a chance, Adam." Brian points to the stinky fish-cleaning station we are passing at Snug Harbor.

The road becomes curvy, and we're covered in dark shadows from a thick stand of tall trees at our side. Mom was right, it's chilly on the ride, and I'm glad I've got my sweatshirt on.

Stopping for traffic to clear before we cross the road, we pedal onto South Peterson. The bike path has ended now, and we are single file on the narrow country road. We pump our way up hills and push hard on the small, bendy slopes. The journey continues. "Do you need to rest?" Mom asks.

"Not yet," Brian calls out.

"Not, me." I sit high in the seat and enjoy the wind on my face. Farmland is all around me as I watch the tops of cornstalks gently sway from side to side.

We turn at West River Road, jog onto North Weber and then onto Michillinda. It's one bumpy country road after another. I pump harder, puffing for breath. The top of my thigh muscles begins to tingle.

"Just one and a half miles west on this road," Brian says. "Then it's only a half mile to go."

This trip is starting to feel like five trips to Lake Hills School, but I pedal onward. Then, up ahead, another hill. And, it looks worse than the killer Block House hill. It is a long, steady, upward slope. I wish I had my lucky conch shell to make this ride magically easy.

I take a deep breath and pedal harder. The tingling in my legs turns to burning. I gasp and try to take in more air. Now my legs no longer burn – they're numb. I raise myself off the bike seat, standing up to pedal with more power. I'm determined. I can do this!

We turn onto Zeller Road and the blueberry patch is in sight! Yahoo! I feel like a horse that catches sight of the barn door and knows he's in the home stretch.

Steering our way into the berry patch, we hop off our bikes. My legs barely hold me up and I plop onto the ground.

Then I hear kids. Twenty pairs of feet stomping as kids my size race wildly through the berry patch yelling out, "Giant! Wizard! Dwarf!"

It's a game of tag I recognize from school.

I sit up to get a better look. Getting to my feet, I discover my legs are no longer wobbly. And I remember I did the ride all on my own, without needing luck.

My eyes scan Palmer's farmland, searching for the game of tag in progress. That's when I see her – a girl about my age. But she is not with the other kids in the berry patch. In fact, she stands with one foot tapping, like she's waiting for something. Slowly, the girl starts to sway from side to side. A mellow tune seeps from her lips as she hums a song. I scratch my head. There isn't any singing when you play giants, wizards, and dwarfs.

Behind me, weaving in and out of the thick blueberry bushes, kids chase one another. Their shouts echo throughout the berry patch. But the toe-tapping girl seems to be off in a world of her own. I wonder why she isn't playing tag.

Suddenly, she looks up at me, her bright blue eyes flash and she smiles.

I take a few steps closer and ask, "Are you a giant, wizard, or dwarf?"

"I'm none of those. I'm a mermaid," she says with certainty, her brilliant blue eyes firmly on mine.

"But, there's no mermaids in this game," I say politely, trying not to hurt the girl's feelings.

"I know," she says. "But I can still be a mermaid, queen of the sea." Her dazzling blue eyes dance as her whole face lights up. This little girl knows who she is and what she wants. She marches away with pride.

Mom's cell phone rings and the chirp turns my head. She waves me over.

"Hello? I see. Drive a little farther. Okay, hold the line," she says into the phone. Then she covers the phone with her hand and says to Brian and me, "It's Papa, he waited forty minutes and now he's at the jog in the road on West River. He's wondering why he hasn't found us yet."

"He thinks we can't peddle all the way here," I whisper. "Let's surprise him."

"Yeah, we'll make him think we didn't make it," Brian says in a giggly, hushed voice.

Mom plays along and says into the phone, "Just keep going. Drive a little farther."

We sneak into the blueberry patch. "No, we're not lost. Keep driving." Mom is still leading Papa on.

Moments later, we hear truck tires crunch on the gravel driveway. I recognize Papa's shadow in the driver seat because he's wearing his fedora.

"Surprise!" we yell, bursting from the berry patch.

Papa gets out of the truck and scratches his head. "Never thought you could pedal this far. Near-enough ten miles."

After picking our buckets of berries, we load the bikes into the truck and drive back to the state park.As we pull into the campsite, Grandma is waiting for us.

"Did you pedal all the way, Adam?" she asks.

"Sure thing. It was *easy*," I say.

At the sound of that word, Grandma has a twinkle in her eye, and I know our secret is safe with her. But then I realize I want to be more like the girl who was proud to be a mermaid of her own making. I need to have the courage to be myself and speak the truth.

With shoulders squared and head held high, I say, "Actually Grandma, it was a tough ride. Just like our sand dune hike was tough."

"And you're a better man because of it, Adam," Grandma says with pride.

Yes, I am.

Chapter 13

Open Mouth, Insert Foot

"Hello ... anybody here?"

Huh? I hop out of bed, blinking and stumbling around. The clock in the camper kitchen glares at me. Somehow, I've managed to sleep till ten. I rub my eyes and take a closer look around. The camper is empty. Where are Mom and Brian? Just a moment later, someone appears.

"Hello? Hello, Sweetie! Can I come in?" It's Freckles, calling from outside, but I can't imagine what she's doing at our campsite.

"No, wait a minute ... um ... um," I mutter, still half asleep but realizing that I'm in an old pair of yellow soccer shorts with "Dude" printed on one leg. Instantly my face feels warm.

"I can't hear you. I'll just come in," Freckles says.

Quickly I peek out the window. She's getting off her bike and walking to the camper screen door. Jeepers. I can't let her see me in these silly shorts. She is certain to tease me. My heart starts beating triple time. I want to hide under a bed – but the bed here in the camper is also the kitchen table, folded flat, and there is no space to crawl under it. There is only one thing to do. I squeeze into the tiny bathroom and lock the door. Even for me, being broomstick skinny, there isn't much room to turn around between the tiny sink and super-narrow shower. I hope I don't have to be squeezed in here too long.

The metal frame of the screen door clangs, so Freckles must be inside now. Sure enough, I hear her voice right outside the bathroom door, "Hello. Where are you, Sweetie?"

My hammering heart beats like a bass drum. "Uh ... I'm in here," I say, frantically searching for something else to wear, anything better than these silly yellow shorts. The only choices are a plastic shower curtain or Mom's pink shirt hanging on a hook. Even the towel rack is empty, so now I realize that Brian and Mom must be out doing laundry.

We wash clothes once a week at the Muskegon State Park Laundromat. These crummy shorts were the only clean things left when I went to bed last night. I sigh and throw on Mom's pink shirt. At least it covers up "Dude." But, oh no, there is writing on the shirt, too. It reads: "Put Art in Your Heart." Can it get any worse?

Maybe if I fold my arms across my chest, Freckles won't see the words. I glance in the mirror. My hair looks okay, no bed-head because it's trimmed short. At this moment, I have never been happier about that decision, especially since I never keep track of a comb.

Quickly, I splash water on my face, trying to look like I have been up for hours doing push-ups and washing the van and going for a hike.

"Hello, Sweetie, where are you?"

"I'm in the bathroom," I say through the locked door. Catching another glimpse of myself in the mirror wearing Mom's T-shirt, I look like a giant wad of pink bubble gum. I let out a moan. I can't believe this is happening to me.

"So are you sick or something?" Freckles asks. "You okay?"

"No."

"Wait, I don't get it," Freckles says. "No, you're not sick. Or no, you're not okay?

"No, I'm not sick," I say, even though I feel a bit sick because I look like a giant bottle of Pepto Bismol.

"What're you doing in there?" Freckles asks.

"Hiding," I mumble, wishing she would disappear.

"Why?"

"Well …" I say, feeling trapped. What choice do I have but to spill it? "I have on my mom's shirt." There I said it.

"So? Just come out," Freckles says. Then she adds with a purr, "I'm looking for Brian."

Instantly my face feels hot and the mirror confirms that I'm glowing brighter than the pink T-shirt. Since yesterday, everyone has been looking for Brian. Our dad called. Grandma and Papa, too. All because my brother was picked to play on the Little League All-Star team.

During the summer, Brian and I have played Little League baseball on the local team called the Cowboys. Now, at the end of the season, coaches pick a player or two from each local team to play on the regional West All-Star team. Brian was chosen, and now everyone is cheering like he is a champion. It doesn't seem fair I didn't get picked. I can throw a baseball farther than Brian.

With my anger more powerful than my need to stay hidden, I whip open the bathroom door. My arms are stiff at my side, with fists tightened into balls. "Why do you want Brian?" The words spit out of my mouth.

Freckles' mouth drops open and her sharp sea-green eyes fix on me, or rather, on the baggy pink T-shirt. "Put Art in Your Heart" stands out like glow-in-the-dark paint.

"Actually, I'm ..." Freckles starts, but fails to finish her sentence. She fights to hold back giggles, covering her mouth with her hand as she stares.

I cross my arms across my chest, hoping Freckles is a slow reader. But knowing her passion for fashion, Freckles hasn't missed a beat.

"Brian's at the laundromat with my mom," I say, and quickly add, "with all our clothes."

"I'll go wait outside for Brian," Freckles says with a smile as her stinging green eyes take in my bubble gum T-shirt one more time.

"Okey-dokey." What? I never say *okey-dokey*. What a dopey thing to say. Will I get anything right this morning?

The camper door clangs shut as Freckles leaves, but I call to her through the screen, "So why are you looking for Brian?"

"I want to wish him good luck," she purrs, again. She flashes a smile so big it lights up her round face. Even her dimples look happy. "Isn't it heavenly that he's an All-Star?"

"Since when do you care about the All-Star game?" I ask.

"It's just I'm so proud of Brian for making the team." She bats her eyelashes as fast as a hummingbird's wings.

I try to think of something I'm talented at doing. Without much thought, I utter, "Well, did you know I can play a fiddle?" Where did that come from? Why do I blurt out the first thing that comes to my mind? The truth is I have only had a half-hour trumpet lesson where I was taught how to buzz my lips. I haven't even blown air into a trumpet yet. So why would I ever say I can play a fiddle?

"Gosh. That's wonderful," Freckles says. Now she flashes dreamy sea-green eyes at me.

Luckily, Red walks up and interrupts us. "I'm looking for Brian. I heard he's a big star." Oh, boy. Everybody is so excited for my brother. Everybody but me, that is.

"Brian's doing laundry," Freckles says to Red. Then she twirls toward her bike, skirt spinning, pigtails swinging. "I'll come back later to wish him good luck," she says and hops on her bike. "Maybe, then, I can hear you play, Adam." She rides away, her sea-green eyes sparkling in the sun.

Well, who cares about Freckles anyway? Not me. I couldn't care less. There is just one thing I care about. Baseball. I push the screen door open, step outside, and plunk down on the bottom camper step.

Sitting down next to me, little Red returns to what the girl was saying. "What are ya gonna play, Adam?"

"Freckles thinks I can play a fiddle."

"That's great," Red says.

"Except I can't play a fiddle, a violin, or even a kazoo. I don't make the spelling bee, and I don't make the All-Star baseball team. I'm plain and boring," I say.

"Well, I can't do those things either, and I don't feel boring," Red says.

"Yeah, but you're five years old. I'm older. I should be able to do something special."

"And ya told Freckles ya can play the fiddle?" Red asks.

I nod, hoping if I don't say the fib out loud my nose won't grow long like Pinocchio's.

Getting up from the camper step, the whale-size pink T-shirt hangs over my legs. Well, at least Red is too young to care about my silly outfit. That's at least one less embarrassing thing.

"So, Adam, why aren't ya on the All-Star team?" Red asks.

"I'm not old enough." Another fib slips out of my mouth. Why am I doing this? First the fiddle fib, and now the baseball lie about being too young. At this rate, I'll beat Pinocchio by a wooden yardstick.

I hang my head. I don't know why I didn't get picked for the All-Star team. I can run the bases faster than a racehorse.

"Can Brian smash home runs? Is that why he got picked?" Red asks.

"Nah, he can't even throw the ball very far." Uh-oh, my Pinocchio nose just grew another inch.

"He can't?"

"Well, he never plays outfield. And most times, I throw the ball farther than Brian." I jump up from the picnic table, sock my hand into a pretend mitt, and then arch my arm like I'm whipping a fastball. "I call my mighty throw a straight-curve ball because it never curves."

"Wow," Red says his eyes wide and round like flying saucers.

"I bet I could throw a ball all the way to the next galaxy," I say.

Red's mouth drops open, rounder than a full moon.

"Yeah. And I like to tease Brian about his wimpy long-distance toss. I tell him it's like a spaghetti noodle, soft and floppy." I take Red's arm and jiggle it like Jell-O.

"But Brian still gets to be a big star?" Red asks.

I nod yes and shuffle over to plop down at the picnic table.

"Well, golly. I think I'll go home. There's not much going on here," Red says and walks toward his campsite. "Call me when Brian gets back."

"Yeah, I'll come get you." I take a deep breath. When I get these "Dude" shorts and goofy pink T-shirt off, maybe then I'll feel like stirring up some fun. Suddenly, I remember my fiddle problem with Freckles. I bonk my head on the picnic table. How can I get out of this mess? A furry brown caterpillar is curled up on the table.

I stretch out my hand and the little critter rolls onto my finger. When I had an ant farm, talking to the ants always comforted me. I find myself doing it again now with the caterpillar.

"Hey, little guy," I say. "Don't you know it's August and you should be a butterfly by now. Did you get left behind like me? I guess we're both having a bad day."

"Are things really that bad?" I say, pretending the bug answers me. I know caterpillars can't talk, but it makes me feel better to make believe.

"You can't imagine what I did this time," I say back to the caterpillar.

"So this is not the first time you've had a problem?" my soft and furry friend asks as he wiggles, tickling my hand.

"No. I've gotten myself in some crummy spots before, but this one is a whopper," I say, cuddling the critter in my palm.

Suddenly, the bug uncurls and stretches out as far as its body will go. More than a hundred legs appear. "Hey, you're not a caterpillar who got left behind, after all."

"That's right. I'm a centipede."

"That's good news for you. Now it's just me and my bad day."

"What's the problem?" the centipede asks.

"I told Freckles I can play the fiddle. But I can't. Now she'll probably tell everyone in the park that I can fiddle.

Heck, by now, everyone in Muskegon probably knows. Maybe even everyone in Michigan," I say as my stomach does a somersault.

"Well, thank goodness Freckles doesn't think you play a violin," the centipede says.

"Yeah, a violin is fancy. I would have to wear a tuxedo and stand up straight."

"That would be worse," the centipede says. "At least fiddling is foot stomping fun."

It feels good to have a kind and comforting friend. I watch the centipede crawl away, wondering what Freckles will say when she finds out I can't play. She probably won't be my friend anymore, and it's my own fault for not telling the truth.

Minutes later, Mom and Brian return with the laundry. Out of the clothes basket, I snag cargo shorts and a plain brown T-shirt. Quickly, I dash into the camper to change.

Brian calls to me from outside, "Throw me some pitches, Adam!" Looking out the camper window, I see he has picked up a baseball bat and is taking a perfect batter's stance, with the bat raised just above his shoulder.

There is nothing better to do, so I head outside and grab a ball and mitt.

"Here it comes!" I say, throwing my special "straight-curve" ball.

The ball whizzes toward Brian, heading straight as an arrow. I smile to myself with pride for my fastball.

Brian smacks it. There is a sweet, solid thunk as the bat kisses leather. I watch the ball skip across the campsite. "Grounder," I say.

Brian doesn't hit home runs. He just whacks the ball a short distance. But Brian's friend Scott Johnson? Boy, can he hit the homers! When Scott's swinging at the plate, he grunts. Once, he snorted so hard that snot came out his nose. Scott is cool. Another time, Scott slugged a ball so hard it cleared the centerfield fence – which is a looong ways. It's easy to see why Scott is on the All-Star team.

"Now, let's go over baseball strategy," Brian says.

This is my favorite part. I make up baseball stories, like puzzles, and Brian's job is to solve them. He says baseball strategy teaches you the smart way to play the game.

I begin my story. "There are two outs, you have a teammate on third, and you're up to bat."

Brian swings his imaginary bat and says, "I hit the ball short, just over the pitcher's head. My teammate runs home and I run like mad to first base." He races around and rams into the dirt, stirring up sand and dust like he's just slid into first. I don't know if I enjoy the story more or watching Brian pretend he's a superstar Chicago Cub rocketing to first base.

Plop! What was that? A drop of water on my arm. Plop! Another drop hits my nose. I look up to see dark clouds hovering all over the state park. In seconds, rain begins to beat down and we dart into the camper.

"Do you think they'll call off the game?" Brian asks.

I grab Mom's laptop and search for the weather report. Yikes! Radar shows a band of thunderstorms sitting right over the Lake Michigan shore.

"Will the storm pass?" Brian asks, hovering over my shoulder.

"Sure," I say. What am I talking about? I never pay attention to an official weather report. If it is raining, I play indoors. If it's nice outside, I play outdoors. Only when Farmer Frank hustled us into a root cellar did I get concerned about weather. But that time, they had announced a tornado watch.

"Adam, can you tell how fast the storm is moving?" Brian asks. "The game is scheduled to start in two hours, forty-three minutes."

"I can't tell how fast it's moving," I say. "I just see a blob of yellow right on top of us."

Outside it's raining so hard that water pours off the awning and forms a trench of water, like a castle moat, in the sand. In no time at all, the entire campground will become one giant puddle. Now worried about his game, Brian shuffles to the back of the camper, his head hanging low. I type like mad on the laptop to search for more information. The All-Star game is scheduled to play at Spring Lake High School. It is the first time anyone in our family will play on a full-size, official baseball diamond. I log onto the school website. "Brian, look!" I say. "When you play on an official field, all regulations are followed, and in case of rain, the high school has a ground crew to cover the field with a tarp before the game."

Brian rushes to my side and reads the screen. "I have an idea, Adam. Go back to the weather map," he says.

I click back to the correct page. The yellow cluster over Lake Michigan is brighter than a caution traffic light. Brian leans in close.

"Look. See that blue box? Click there," he says, pointing to a spot labeled *Extended Forecast*.

I click, and the screen changes into bars and graphs – an hour-by-hour weather report.

"By 7 p.m. the thunderstorm warning ends," Brian reads. "The field will be dry by the 8 p.m. start time and we can play ball!" Joyfully, he tosses his mitt into the air. Thump. The mitt whacks the camper's low ceiling and hits the floor with a thud. "Oops, forgot I was inside." Brian scoops up his mitt and skips out the screen door, staying under the awning and out of the downpour.

At dusk, we pile into the van and drive to the high school. The rain stopped more than an hour ago and an army of men are yanking 80 feet of tarp off the infield. As they heave, water rolls off the canvas. Behind them, dust flies. The infield is bone dry! And it is marked for Little League – 60 feet in dimension.

I look up to see hundreds of outdoor lights shining down on the field. It's so bright, I could use sunglasses.

Only a short while later, the teams are called out onto the field in this big East against West game. The announcer begins to introduce individual players. Through the stadium speakers, I hear Brian's name ring across the field. The announcer's booming voice makes it sound really important. In his uniform, wearing Number 7, Brian jogs out to join his team. Then we stand to sing the national anthem. This really is an All-Star game.

I settle in the packed bleachers with Mom to cheer for West, Brian's team. The ballpark is filled with noise from the shoulder-to-shoulder crowd in the stands.

East's star player is up to bat. "B-a-a-a-a-ck up," Mom says, sounding like a sheep. A hot glow creeps across my face. I wish she'd be like the other parents and shout, "Hey, batter, batter!"

Among the chants, the game carries on. Brian is playing second. He punches his fist into his mitt, waiting for a ball to come his way. Surprisingly soon – whack! The well-hit grounder rolls right for Brian like a firecracker on a short fuse. He scoops it up and whips it to first. No spaghetti arm when he plays infield. It's a close call for the umpire.

"Safe!" he shouts.

Mom and I groan, but there is more than one throw to a game.

We keep rooting for West. The scoreboard glows in the evening light. It's been a back-and-forth game all the way, and now it's the top of the sixth– the final inning in Little League – and West is at bat with the score tied at five runs apiece. It is Brian's turn at bat, there's one out, and he has runners on second and third.

Brian taps the bat against his shoe spikes, wraps his hands firmly into place, and cocks the bat perfectly above his shoulder. He stares straight at the pitcher, squinting with powerful focus. I know that Brian is totally in this game, and I quickly say to myself one of our baseball practice strategies: Keep your eye on the ball. Keep your eye on the ball.

East's pitcher, a big guy, winds up. His large hand completely covers the ball. Then, like a cannon, he fires off a pitch and it sails toward the plate. What a fast pitch! Usually a pitcher's arm gets tired in the last inning, but not this kid's.

Swish! Strike one.

Preparing for another power-busting throw, the pitcher anchors his step, grinds his back foot into the sand, and lifts his forward leg. He arches his big arm behind his head. The ball whips through the air. Another fastball at my brother. Strike two.

I think about the strategy. "Focus on the pitch," I say under my breath.

The pitcher spits to the side, then rubs the ball hard between his hands. He grits his teeth, arches his arm again, and thrusts the ball with a mighty spin.

Crack! Brian's bat connects with the ball! Not a home run. Not a long drive to the outfield. But almost as good at this spot in the game. It is just a short, consistent hit – and it means a runner will easily advance to home. Brian sprints toward first, his legs moving faster than a jackrabbit's to try to beat the throw and get on base.

The crowd stands and roars, with whistling and yelling and clapping all around the ballpark. "Yes! One run in," I say and pump my fist in the air. West takes the lead, but Brian doesn't make first in time. "Out!" the umpire hollers. Brian scuffs the dirt as he heads back to the dugout.

That's two outs.

Next at bat for West is "Home Run" Scott. The crowd cheers and chants, "Homer! Homer! Homer!" I stand up, but I'm unsure what to cheer. On the way to the game, in the van, I bragged about Scott's home runs and Brian said, "We're on opposite sides about home runs."

"Huh?" I said.

"You think homers are everything. I don't," Brian said.

"You don't?" I asked. "Why not?"

"If you swing for outside the box every time, you'll strike out more often than you get a home run. Or you'll get walked. And that doesn't help the team much."

It turns out there isn't much time for me to decide if I should join the shouting crowd or not. With all his might, Scott swings at every pitch – and strikes out. West retires and now the other team, East, has the last at bat for the game.

I remember what Brian had told me in the van. "Base hits" are the key, he said.

Thinking base hits are pretty dull stuff, I had asked him why he thought they were so good.

"A player who can place hits here and there around the field is a player who is worth something to a team."

"Huh?"

"If you can get hits, you'll get runners on bases. And that can bring a teammate home. Plus, if you can place a hit in different spots, it keeps the other team guessing."

"Okay," I said at the time but shrugged my shoulders, too.

East gets ready to bat. Their fans are on their feet, yelling and shouting and begging their first batter to smash the ball. "Homer, homer, homer!" echoes through the stands. They want to win this game, badly.

Their first batter swings wildly at every pitch, slicing air each time and striking out.

East's second player steps up to the plate.

"Homer, homer, homer!" The crowd continues.

The second batter swings fiercely. The bat kisses a piece of the ball, sending it straight up in the air. The pop fly is caught. That's two outs.

By now, not a single person in the bleachers remains seated. As we stomp our feet, the metal bleachers echo a clang louder than thunder. East fans shout for the homer. West fans roar for the out.

The third batter is at the plate. He swings so hard he spins in a full circle as he misses the ball. That's strike one.

"Homer, homer, homer!" The East fans clearly don't share Brian's baseball strategy.

Next pitch, the batter swings full force. Strike two.

My ears buzz from the rumble of noise.

The pitcher winds up and fires the ball. The batter slashes at the pitch, but the ball keeps going and smacks cleanly into the catcher's mitt. Strike three. Hooray! West lands the victory!

Back in the van and bouncing in our seats, we cheer and retell Brian's baseball tips and strategies all the way home. My brother is not the smash-the-ball-out-of-the-park kind of player, but now I understand why he was picked to be an All-Star.

We pull up to the campsite and see that Red is sitting on top of the picnic table. Well, almost sitting, his feet move so fast it's like he is doing a tap dance on the seat. "Who won?" he asks before we can even get out of the van.

"West! We did!"

"Yippee! I knew Brian could do it!" Red says and jumps up and down. Then he stops. He turns to me, and whispers, "Hey Adam, I haven't heard nothing about a fiddle."

"That's good," I say quietly. Maybe it's my lucky day, and Freckles hasn't blabbed it all over the campground.

Red leans in close to me and murmurs in my ear, "Then I talked to Freckles."

I feel my heart thump beneath my ribs. Yet before Red can say any more; Freckles rides up on her bike. My palms turn sweaty. But before I can blink, she beelines to Brian. "Who won the game?" she asks.

"We did," he beams, with his chest puffed out.

"Oh, how lovely," Freckles says, voice gooey like honey. Then she steps away and looks straight at me with her stormy sea-green eyes.

All I hear is the thump-thump of my heart. I figure it is best to confess the truth. "Red said you talked to him about the fiddle," I say.

Instantly she lowers her eyes to the ground and her cheeks glow pinker than her dress. "I should have told you it's not my favorite instrument."

"Yeah, she was never gonna ask ya to play, Adam," Red pipes up.

Suddenly, I'm safe. Freckles is not going to tell anyone about my fiddle fib. Then Mom asks, "What fiddle? Were you stretching tall tales again, Adam?"

Just as quickly, I strike out. Mom, Freckles, Brian, and Red all stare at me. But it is Freckles to speak first.

"No, nothing quite that serious," Freckles says. I can't believe it … she's covering for me.

Freckles really is my friend.

Then Brian says, "Yeah, Adam is good at making up stories for me, too. We use them to run baseball practice plays."

And my brother is my hero.

Chapter 14

A Trick from a Cowboy

Before a big black fly landed smack onto my cereal.

Before Brian ate the last jelly doughnut.

Before Mom reminded me it was the last day of our vacation, I was having another great morning of camping. Now, my day is falling apart, realizing that tomorrow, Mom will head to her home in North Dakota while Brian and I will go back to Dad's in Spring Lake. And then, it's school again. Yuck. I wish time could stand still. Why can't we camp forever? I grab a baseball cap and slap it on my head. Life just feels better wearing a ball cap.

"Since it's the last day of Moynihan family vacation, I'll let you two pick what we should do," Mom says to Brian and me.

This is a struggle. I could pick leaping and creeping through the tall weeds as we snatch grasshoppers. Or maybe romping and stomping in the sand dunes as we shoot slingshots. What a curse to have to pick just one.

"Let's make invisible ink," Brian suggests.

Invisible ink? My brother stuns me. Why stay indoors when the wild wilderness is at our doorstep?

"How about an *outdoor* sport!" I wave my hand at the sunbeams streaming through the camper window and hope I can distract Brian from another indoor activity. There are so many outdoor adventures yet to be had, and this camping trip is almost over. Doesn't he remember school will start soon and there will be plenty of time for indoor stuff like trumpet lessons and Cub Scouts?

Then I recall when school starts we play league soccer – outside. And Mom always comes to our first game. She comes to see us every time the calendar turns to a new month, never missing a trip. My day begins to brighten again until I hear Brian say, "We have everything we need for invisible ink. Vinegar, cornstarch, and lemon juice."

Mom sees my smile fade. "I have an idea," she says. "Throw your favorite activity into a hat, shake it up, and we'll draw out the winner."

We get out two pieces of paper. Brian writes – I don't know what he writes. But I write one of my favorites. We dump the papers into the ball cap. I close my eyes, mix them up and get ready to pick one.

At first, I think I should take a chance and let luck choose the winner. Then a voice whispers in my head,

"Nonsense. It's the last day of vacation. Pick the fun activity." So, I peek a little. Yes, I know it's a mean trick, but the important thing is we'll have fun outside today.

I shake the hat one last time. Just enough so I can see a hint of the first letter of my own handwriting. I reach in, snag the paper, and unfold it. "We're off to the big beach," I say, after reading the activity on the paper.

The big beach is the eastern shoreline of Lake Michigan – miles of sand for digging and miles of water for swimming. Just as much as I do, my brother loves to fight the waves of the surf and build skyscraper sand castles. Plus, this beach has the only snack bar in the park. And it has Brian's favorites – bubblegum ice cream and cherry Twizzlers – so I don't feel badly for peeking and picking the beach.

"I'll grab the Little Blue Purse," Brian says, knowing the beach snack bar is the only place we can spend coins from the special purse – a small leather pouch the size of a wadded up sweat sock. Mom packs it on every camping vacation.

Brian grabs the Little Blue Purse and gives it a shake. The jingling of coins makes him grin as big as the Kool-Aid Pitcher guy. He doesn't seem disappointed about the invisible ink.

Mom's head turns to the sound of the coins rattling in the Little Blue Purse. "Aren't you glad I save my loose change all year so we can buy beach treats?" she asks.

249

"It's my favorite tradition," I say, patting my tummy.

Brian unzips the leather pouch and counts out the coins. "We're down to one dollar and eighty-five cents for each of us," he reports. Each time we use the purse, Brian gives us a rundown of its remaining contents by dividing the sum of the coins into the number of camping days left. Oh, boy. I think he'll be the treasurer of the State of Michigan someday or hold some other fancy job doing math.

Oh, well. What matters now is I have enough money to buy a small popcorn and a pack of M&Ms. I like to mix the chocolate with the popcorn. "Mmm," I say, smacking my lips as I imagine the aroma of buttered popcorn.

"Adam, quit daydreaming," Brian says. Jeepers. How does he do that? He can always tell when I get sidetracked.

"Thinking about my chocolaty-salty snack invention," I say.

"Ick, you mix the craziest combinations." Brian sticks out his tongue and gags.

"At least I'm not plain and boring like you," I say. "You use a dinner plate with dividers so your food won't mix together."

My brother is quick to sling a zinger back. "It's better than thinking jelly doughnuts are a food group, Adam."

"Hey-hey, you two," Mom says. "Let's load up the beach gear."

Inside the camper, Brian and I are packing cold drinks in the cooler when the park ranger strolls up and calls into the camper.

"Hey, Ranger," I say thru the screen door. It is the same man who has come almost daily. His green uniform has nifty badges and medals that flash in the sun.

"You boys are the only fellows I know who get snail-mail at this campground. You must be pretty important," he says, waving an envelope.

"Yup! And we love getting letters from Dad's house," I say, swinging open the screen door to take the envelope.

"Adam, it's a photograph, not a letter," Brian corrects me.

"Yeah, okay, photograph." I shrug my brother off and snatch the envelope from the ranger as he tips his green park hat, silently saying good-bye. I smile and wave a farewell to our daily visitor.

"So what do you think Meijer will be doing in this photograph?" I ask, thinking about our pet guinea pig at Dad's house. His cage is in the family room, between Brian's bedroom and mine. Each morning, when the sun rises, Meijer wakes up and squeaks. I giggle. There is no need for an alarm clock when you live with this guinea pig.

"I'm not sure what Meijer will be doing. But if you don't open it up, we'll never know," Brian says as he tries to nab the envelope from my hand.

I jerk away to escape his reach. My eyes catch sight of the photograph of Meijer already stuck on the camper refrigerator door.

"Last time, he was reading." I tap that photo of Meijer wearing hilarious eyeglasses on his soft, pink nose and huddling atop a Hardy Boys book.

"Adam, you know guinea pigs can't read, right?" my brother snaps.

"I know, I know."

The photographs are a fun game Dad plays with us, dressing Meijer in silly costumes and putting him in funny situations. My favorite picture is Meijer hugging the Nintendo controller with "Mario Cart" lit up on the video screen in the background. The message says: "I'm playing without you boys."

I rip open the envelope. There's Meijer, wrapped in a bath towel, his light brown furry head peeking out. I read the title, "I went in the hot tub without you. Miss you!"

Jeepers. I know it's just a photograph, but it feels like I can see Meijer's whiskers twitch. I imagine his bright black eyes blinking at me, and I get an empty feeling in my stomach. Seeing Meijer tomorrow is one good thing about going home.

Mom has the van loaded and we drive the short distance to the beach at Lake Michigan.

"Do you think it's a Wet Day or Dry Day?" I ask.

"I don't know. I didn't check the wind direction," Brian says.

"I hope the wind isn't from the north. That wind stirs up the lake, and the water gets so cold it feels like a giant ice cube," I say.

When the northern wind blows, I call it a Dry Beach Day – no swimming. A Wet Beach Day is just the opposite. The wind blows gently from the southwest and pushes all the warm top-water toward shore. On a Wet Day, I dive and glide and splash through the water until my fingers shrivel.

The van pulls into the parking lot. I open the door and feel a slight breeze. The gentle wind pushes the water into an even flow of small waves that gently roll in and out. The sand is hot and squeaks a little song as Brian sprints away to test the water. I help Mom collect the beach gear.

"You're getting to be more like Brian," she says as we carry the cooler and beach tote.

"Gee whiz. I hope not." I suck in a deep breath so I won't freak out. I don't want to be like my brother.

"But you are," Mom says. "For instance, like now, you're being responsible and helping me."

"Well, maybe I can be like him in a few ways," I say.

"By all means, like dependable. And trustworthy," Mom says and gives me a little hug.

"But not his love for broccoli." I scrunch my face and wriggle free. I can't do broccoli. Ditto the all-A's report card.

As I spread out a beach towel, I hear someone call my name.

"Adam! Over here." It's Red.

Out of 147 campsite choices, I am lucky to have Red as my next-door state-park neighbor. His silliness during the vacation makes me laugh, especially his bright red, punk-style hair that stands on end.

But who is that next to him? And what is on that man's head?

"I'll be right over," I call to Red. I tell Mom where I'm headed and then trot the short distance to my friend.

Standing next to Red is a man taller than Dad. In fact, he's enormous. His neck is almost thicker than his head. And his darkened face is rough like a football left out in the rain.

"This is Grandpa Joe," Red says.

"Pleased ta meet ya," Grandpa says with a funny twang in his voice.

I can only stare, not because of his size, but because when he talks he sounds like a country western singer. I am familiar with Papa Schroeder's German accent and rolling "r" way of talking. But this twang is unlike anything I've heard before.

And then there is his hat. I've only seen that kind of cowboy hat in westerns on TV. I tug at the brim of my own ball cap. Its familiarity gives me comfort.

While shaking Grandpa Joe's hand, I realize it isn't at all like mine. His grip covers my entire hand and it's scratchy and scaly like a lizard.

"Grandpa drove from North Dakota to visit me," Red says.

I learn Grandpa Joe sold his farm last winter. This is the first time he's been able to leave his crops and come to Michigan to relax at the beach. Every other summer, going way back, he has been on a tractor in the middle of hundreds of acres of wheat.

"We've enough wheat in North Dakota to fill Lake Michigan," Grandpa Joe says as he casts his arm wide in a dramatic sweep across the big blue water. The lake stretches farther than we can see.

I am glad I don't live in North Dakota. How could I find worms and fish, or catch frogs in an ocean of wheat? Mom lives in North Dakota, but in the city. Grandpa Joe's farm sounds a lot different than where Mom lives.

"Yeow!" The sound of my brother's yelp turns my head. Twenty feet ahead, Brian looks like he's doing a jig. And it's not hot coals that make him jump. Only the frigid water of Lake Michigan makes you do that dance – which tells me it's a Dry Beach Day. Gosh, being unable to swim, maybe I won't feel so sad going home tomorrow.

In the echoes of Brian's hoo-ha, I hear Mom call me. "Come get the suntan oil," she says, waving a brown plastic bottle she gets in the beauty department.

I stiffen ram-rod straight at her words. When Mom smears that suntan oil on my skin, it slides across like slime and leaves a slippery film. Worse yet, I smell like a fruity coconut.

"Adam, you'll get burned," Mom calls again.

What can I do? I have to act fast to avoid this disaster. Uncertain, my eyes dart in every direction, and then I see Red's beach bag. I snatch a tube of sports cream and wave it in the air like an S.O.S. signal. "I'll use some of Red's," I say, squirting some on.

"Fine by me." With that said, Mom settles in with a book.

What a close call. Yet, I'm not sure what the big deal about sunscreen is anyways. My Moynihan-Irish skin must have Papa's German toughness mixed in, because I suntan easily. Not like Red, whose fair skin has two settings – pale or burnt.

Grandpa Joe lowers himself into a squatty beach chair. It's made for the shoreline so you can sit by the water and let the waves lap at your toes. But Grandpa seems comfortable using it in the middle of the sandy beach.

"So, is North Dakota that way?" I ask and point northwest at the endless watery horizon.

"A tad farther west," Grandpa Joe says.

"That's right," says Brian, who has returned from testing the water. "It's 118 miles here to cross Lake

Michigan to Wisconsin. Then he also passes through Minnesota before getting to North Dakota."

"You betcha," Grandpa Joe says and nods to Brian.

"This is my brother, Brian," I say. "And Brian, this is Red's Grandpa Joe."

"So you're a newcomer to Lake Michigan?" Brian asks.

"Sure enough."

A newcomer to the beach – I repeat it in my mind – what a treasure! "Hey matey!" I say, turning to Red and feeling like a pirate. "Let's bury Grandpa Joe in the sand."

"Aye, aye, captain." Red smiles and grabs a shovel.

"Don't forget the most important step," I say.

"The trench?" Red whispers.

"Yo-ho-ho. That's it," I quietly snicker, covering my mouth to hide the giggles. Scooping a trench is a trick I learned long ago. It lets you pile a lot more sand on top of the person you're going to bury. We don't tell Grandpa Joe, though. It's a pirate's secret.

In the meantime, Grandpa Joe snoozes to the soothing sounds of the water. Every once in a while, he lifts an eyelid and watches the waves steadily, gently reach the shore.

We work quietly, shoveling out piles of sand. We keep the Pirate Code of Honor by not saying a word to Grandpa Joe. It's so much fun to have a newcomer to the beach. This is one secret activity I will surely miss when I have to go home tomorrow. I wish time could stand still.

"One more scoop and the trench will be complete," Brian says.

"Hey, Grandpa, we want to bury ya in the sand. It's a Michigan tradition. Come lay down," Red says and pats the trench.

"I reckon I will," Grandpa Joe says as he eases out of his chair and lies down in the hole. Hooray. The trench swallows him up.

"Put your hands at your sides," I say, trying not to snicker. Grandpa Joe has no idea what it's like to be buried alive in Lake Michigan sand. And of course, dead men tell no tales.

"Hold still," Red says. Grandpa Joe relaxes in the trench. He closes his eyes and enjoys the warm sun on his face. No need to blindfold this prisoner because he's cooperating without a struggle.

"I'll go fetch the water." I sprint to the lake and fill two buckets to the brim. As I race back, water sloshes over the edge of the pails.

Meanwhile, back at the trench, Brian starts to prepare the Pirate's Brew by filling a pail half-full of sand. "Pour in a little bit of water," Brian says. Then with a shovel he begins to mix the sand-water combination. The sand turns darker as the brew sticks together.

"That brew looks perfect for covering the prisoner ... ah, I mean ... Grandpa," I say. Brian stirs the brew once more and then passes it to Red.

"Here comes the sand," Red says to Grandpa Joe as he packs the wet sand around him.

"How are you doing?" I ask Grandpa Joe.

"Fine as cream gravy," he says, using what I think is cowboy slang.

"More water, Adam," Brian says. "We need to mix another batch of brew."

"It's all hands on deck," I shout and dash for more buckets of water. Instantly, it's a fire brigade system. I haul water, Brian mixes brew, and Red packs.

Thump, thump, the sand is packed on Grandpa's legs. Three more buckets of Pirate's Brew cover his chest and shoulders. Soon every inch of Grandpa Joe is covered, except his head, of course.

My eyes shift toward Red and I bellow a low, deep, "Hardee, har, har!"

The pirate snicker forces Red into a grin. Brian laughs, too. The best part is next.

"Fire in the hole!" I yell the pirate's warning.

Red nods at my signal. "Try to get out Grandpa Joe," he says.

Grandpa grunts and yanks his neck forward. But the sand stays packed. "Whoa there, little fellow. This is tough," Grandpa says. He is wrapped up tight as a mummy. "I'll try my legs," Grandpa says. Nothing. "Humph. By hook or by crook, I'll get out. Oomph."

Grandpa tries to move but the sand doesn't loosen. "I'm a goner," Grandpa sighs.

Now it's time for the second-best part about burying a newcomer.

"Okay buccaneers, let's blow the man down!" I snicker and then jog to get Mom's sunglasses and return seconds later.

Red puts Mom's pink sunglasses on Grandpa Joe. The stems won't fit behind his ears. His face is too big, so the glasses slide down his nose, and his eyes peek over the lenses.

"He needs yer baseball cap, Adam." Red giggles as I flip the cap onto Grandpa Joe's head. Sure enough, it's too small, too.

"Don't forget this," Brian says and whips out the straw from a juice box. I stick the straw in Grandpa Joe's mouth, but not quite up his nose. I can't be that mean. After all, he is Red's grandpa.

Poor Grandpa Joe. The straw in his mouth twitches. The pink sunglasses droop down his nose. And the wee-little hat doesn't even protect his head from the sun. He grunts and struggles again. He can't move.

"Okay, you-all have had your fun. Get a wiggle on and get me out of here," Grandpa says. The jig is up."

Shiver me timbers, that's pirate slang for surprise. And not a good surprise. Grandpa Joe's funny twang has an ugly bite to it. His head sweats, and his breathing is deeper, huskier. Grandpa Joe is a big man. What if he has a big mean temper and blindfolds us and makes us walk the plank?

Suddenly, I don't want time to stand still. I think, maybe I should go home – now!

"Don't worry, the sun is hot. It'll dry out the wet sand and it'll crack," Brian says.

Whew. Brian's wise words might save the day. "Look, there's a tiny crack already," I say, trying to cool off Grandpa Joe's anger. "Try to wiggle one more time."

"Oomph," Grandpa Joe says and grunts his teeth. The tiny crack grows a tad wider.

"Jiggle again," I say.

"Rrrghh," he says. The crack splits open, but piles of sand still cover Grandpa Joe's chest and arms and legs.

Quickly, I'm on my knees clawing at the sand with my hands. "Help me, you guys," I say to Brian and Red. Sand flies as we unbury our treasure. Minutes later, all three of us grab Grandpa's hands and tug with all our might. He shoots out of the sand pit. Off flies the ball cap, pink glasses and juice box straw. Grandpa Joe stumbles a little getting his sea legs steady in the sand.

"That was a hog-tying good time!" he bellows, slapping on his cowboy hat and laughing, belly loose, mouth wide. His hearty chuckle chases away my fear and makes me laugh, too.

Sand clings to Grandpa Joe's body. He tries to brush it off, but it sticks like glue. "Go swimming," Red says.

Oh no! Red doesn't know it's a Dry Beach Day! "Wait, the water is ..." I start say.

But Grandpa Joe is too fast. He dashes off to the lake. He whips off his cowboy hat and, with a rowdy splash, plunges into that ice cold water. I knew I should have gone home earlier!

We chase after Grandpa, stopping at the shoreline. His arms flap in a wild walrus rage.

"Rrrghh," he growls, snorting like a cowboy who's been double-crossed. He stands up, rising out of the freezing water. He takes two giant steps toward us and then drips arctic-cold water onto our bare feet.

My heart leaps around in my chest. Grandpa Joe's face is red, and that mean-ugly look is back. I'm glad he's not in the cowboy movies, because if he had a sheriff's badge, he might arrest us.

"Burr!" Grandpa Joe roars. "That's mighty brisk water."

I want to run away, but my legs won't move. Grandpa Joe's huge hand whips by me as he snatches up a beach towel lying on the sand. He begins to dab himself dry when, suddenly, he snaps the towel into the air and uses it as a lasso to rope us toward him. Before I can blink, he gives us a big cowhand hug.

"But, you know what, about that water?" Grandpa Joe says and points to the Big Lake. "It's not as cold as the Missouri River. Just wait till you guys come visit me in North Dakota." Grandpa Joe grins and shakes off a shiver. My racing heart settles down.

Mom calls out that it's time to head back to camp. Brian and I gather our things and wave farewell to our new friend. We help Mom load the van. Having spent my dollar and eighty-five cents from the Little Blue Purse, I sadly crunch my salty M&M-popcorn snack as Mom drives us to the campsite one last time. And so ends the last day of our camping adventures together. Saying good-bye to Mom tomorrow morning will make my stomach feel like I ate too many jelly doughnuts. But Mom says the ache in my belly is real love – being able to feel the sad times, and the happy ones, too. And there will be happy times ahead.

All during vacation, Mom has been saying Brian and I will be old enough to visit her home in the city next summer. And Grandpa Joe invited us to North Dakota, too. I can't wait to discover the West. I imagine myself high in the saddle riding a horse across acres of wheat, like he described.

Now I'm glad time doesn't stand still after all. Instead, with a smile on my face, I dream about the next adventure.

Epilogue

Twenty Years Later

Brian graduated from Michigan Tech University. While attending college he joined Sigma Pi fraternity, making loyal friendships and becoming president of the group. He vows there are no secret codes or passwords in the society.

Today he is a civil engineer studying soil mixtures and building under-structures. His math is beyond Einstein's $E=mc^2$. He lives in Grand Rapids, Michigan working for Soil and Materials Engineering, Inc.

Married to his high school sweetheart, he now has a new favorite role: "The Dad Show." Whether it's hide-and-seek or fort building with his young daughter and son, Brian's Dad show is the top of the hit parade.

Adam attended Michigan State University and is now in the northern mountains of California living off the grid which is crazier than *any* camping adventure. He helps construct farms by operating bull dozers and land graders to form deep lakes for rain water collection. This process of water harvesting, along with building energy stations fueled by sun power, fills his passion for ecology.

On weekends, Adam leaves his tent and off-road vehicle with its monster-size quad tires behind and heads to the excitement of the city – San Francisco. Rooting for the Giants, he is a loyal fan at the games. He plays Pro-Am Beach Soccer and other times he relaxes listening to music at jazz clubs.

When it snows, Adam will bust out spins and flips on his snowboard at the slopes in Lake Tahoe. He can now do that 360!

About the Author - Illustrator

After thirteen years as a registered nurse, Kate
Moynihan returned to college to follow her creative
dreams as an artist. She now paints using watercolor
on paper and oil paints on canvas. For Kate, the bigger
the canvas the better. One time, she painted a picture so
big it didn't fit through the doorway for delivery. Plan B
was to rebuild it outside.

Kate is most famous for birch tree landscapes. She
has created more than a hundred paintings. Each
one is different and yet represents her Michigan birth
place.

In 1993 she moved to Holland, Michigan and opened
a gallery. The store is in the hub of the city shopping
district so her paintings are displayed with all the fun
things that mix with art, home and life.

267

You will find Kate painting in the studio of the store engaging customers while she works. Her love of people and all the silly things they do inspires Kate's spirit. Her passion for learning has never ended, hence her latest project of illustrating and writing her first book sparked by memories of her fun-loving family.

Web site address: www.moynihangallery.com/